8621

DATE DUE

APR. 2 1 2001			

J   8621

Cohen, Peter Zachary
Calm horse, wild night

Calm Horse,

Wild Night

CALM HORSE, WILD NIGHT

Peter Zachary Cohen

1982 ATHENEUM New York

LIBRARY OF CONGRESS CATALOGING IN PUBLICATION DATA

Cohen, Peter Zachary.
Calm horse, wild night.

SUMMARY: A fourteen-year-old places himself in
a very compromising situation
in order to prevent his huge, gentle timber horse
from becoming part of a smuggling scheme.
[1. Smuggling—Fiction. 2. Horses—Fiction]
I. Title.
PZ7.C663Cal   [Fic]   82-1746
ISBN 0-689-30918-X   AACR2

Copyright © 1982 by Peter Zachary Cohen
All rights reserved
Published simultaneously in Canada by
McClelland & Stewart, Ltd.
Composition by American–Stratford Graphic Services, Inc.
Brattleboro, Vermont
Printed and bound by
Fairfield Graphics, Fairfield, Pennsylvania
Designed by Mary M. Ahern
First Edition

Contents

v

PART THREE   Into the Forest, to the Moon

PART FOUR   Moonlight Emergencies

PART FIVE   Doing Different Things Differently

ONE

A World
of Stumps

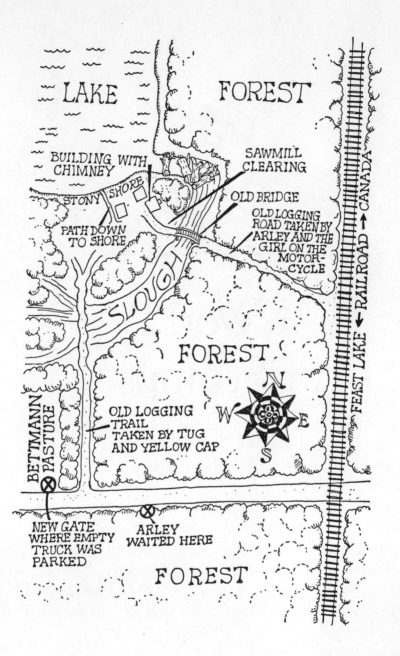

1

The Horse with Horns

ALONG THE EDGE OF the clearing—the edge that was farthest from the road—the chain saw started again. In the warm, windless mid-July air, its ferocious snarling was loud and sudden. Of course that didn't distract Tug any. He'd already started to cross the clearing toward the loading bunk beside the road.

As usual there was no guarantee that he would get there, because the trees that had been growing where the clearing now was had all been fairly young and therefore fairly small. Consequently the thin stumps that remained everywhere were all quite close together. They made Tug seem even taller and rangier than he actually was, and they made it almost impossible for him to drag a sled loaded with six newly cut logs to the road. It was almost like trying to pull a bone through a dog's mouth.

Ordinarily trails would have been grubbed among the stumps in order to move the cut logs to where a big truck could pick them up. And since the stumps were all freshly cut, with their buried roots still strong, that would've required a lot of expensive bulldozer work, or dynamite. But Tug had always managed to get the sled through without special trails, so they had never been made. Pretty soon, as he encountered the tight fits among the stumps again, he was shifting to the side, then lurching back, then stomping forward at an angle from the direction he had been heading. If your eye had been like a telescope and it had focused only on him, he would've looked as drunk as a horse could get.

He was as tall as a short moose, and a third heavier. He had strangely thin ears that stuck up alertly like the horns of an antelope, and the worn metal hames on his padded leather harness collar curved upward noticeably, as if an extra pair of horns were growing out of his shoulders. He was old enough that the hollows above his eyes had sunken in deeply; so he appeared to have two sets of eyes, one above the other. Some light tan netting hung over his back to shake as he moved and help chase off flies; it looked like a great patch of old skin coming loose.

But in all his eighteen years Tug had never given any concern to his appearance. Starting when he'd been four years old, he'd learned the business of "snaking" logs out of the woods. He'd learned to do it well; and always after pulling for a while, he'd found food and water and shelter waiting for him. He'd always earned his keep, and he'd been lucky. None of the men that had had control of him had ever treated him badly. After the time—when he'd been just three years old—when he'd first learned what bridles and harness and reins were for, he'd never had much cause to get excited, and he'd never learned to fear anything.

So when an unfamiliar farm truck went slowly by on the road beside the clearing, he hardly gave it a glance.

Even when the chain saw paused for a moment, and in that moment Tug's thin ears told him that the truck, once it had followed the road out of sight amid the forest, had slowed to a stop, he gave it no more than the merest extra flicker of his ears.

And when the chain saw began snarling again behind him, and when a small group of crows suddenly flew cawing out of the woods near where the truck had gone, Tug still put his main attention on the expert shifting and backing and strong stomping and smooth stepping he had to do in order to keep the logs moving and free from jam-ups amid the stumps.

As was now usual, the fourteen-year-old boy walking beside the logs kept an easy grip on the long, thick leather reins and said little.

2

The Challenge of the
Bull's Face

B<small>Y THEN THEY HAD</small>
come again to a place in the stumpy clearing that
the boy was calling, "Taurus." He used that name
because for most of his life he'd lived on the plains
where trees were scarce and the sky was wide, and
Taurus was one of the constellations he remembered
seeing twinkling at night. The stars of Taurus
formed a long V in the sky that was supposed to
represent the face and horns of a great white bull
that was said to be Zeus, the king of the gods, in
disguise.

7

The stumps that formed his "Taurus" in the clearing left a long V-shaped opening where Tug could pull straight on smooth, slick grass for fifty or sixty yards without any obstacles. But the price for that easy going was ten yards of tense maneuvering where the stumps narrowed together and grew extra thickly. If the log load got jammed there, it would have to be unloaded to be freed, and the wedged sled could easily be cracked by a hard pull in the wrong direction.

The boy took a deep breath as they moved closer to that narrows, and he tried to judge if he needed to rein Tug to the left or right a little, and decided that, as usual, Tug was lining himself up about as good as could be done. The boy thought of giving out a brief word of encouragement, but as usual decided that Tug wouldn't understand the words and to speak might only confuse him.

Tug began pulling and sidestepping into the tight passages. The boy jumped back and forth behind the sled so he could see when it was starting to crowd a stump too closely; then with a silent twitch of the reins, he could let Tug know when to shift away.

The boy's name was Arley Rawlinson, and he never had got the habit of saying much. That was because he had so many thoughts going on inside him and got to feeling so strongly about the things he might want to speak about, that words rarely seemed plentiful or accurate enough.

He could still remember, for example, that time —five years ago—when his dad had taken him aside and told him that Reva and Rosie and all the other cows they owned had gotten a kind of tuberculosis called Bang's disease and would have to be killed, all at once, so the sickness wouldn't spread to other people's herds.

He could remember that time—four years ago— when Dad had taken him aside to say that the money they'd gotten for slaughtering their cows wasn't enough to pay for good ones to replace them, and because of that their calves wouldn't be worth much, and so they were going to have to sell out and move away from their home.

He could also remember a time—now three years ago—when they'd come here, off the open sunny plains into the thick and often cloudy woods around the town of Feast Lake. They'd moved onto a place that was so grown over and shaded with young trees that there wasn't enough grass on all of it to graze five cows.

"That's why it's cheap enough that we can buy it," Dad and Mom had both told him. "But when the trees are cut and hauled off, the grass will grow. And we can sell the trees for pulp to make paper. That's how we'll get back on our feet."

He'd thought a lot about all that, and he'd *felt* about it. And still what was there to say?

And then Dad had come back to their new home one day with the biggest horse Arley had ever imagined.

"He's a gift," Dad had said, "from Jeff Raybel" —who was one of their new neighbors.

Mom had been a bit dubious. "Did he also give us a carload of hay to go with him?" she wondered. "I'll bet he'll need five tons a year."

"Now wait," Dad'd said. "He's not going to be dead weight. Jeff would still be using this horse, except that he's logging so many acres he's gone all to those big tractors. But for an outfit our size—"

"*Whose* size?" Mom had interrupted, then she'd laughed a little. She was being mild about it, but she was plainly worried. "I've never seen anything so big. And we don't know anything about him. If he's got a mean streak, he'll hurt one of us, or—"

"Well, I'll bet this—" Dad had interrupted. "That a mean horse wouldn't have lived to be this old around Jeff Raybel. Let's give him a chance. His name's Tug."

When he had nothing else on his mind, Arley could still remember listening to that argument; but right now in the middle of the stumpy clearing, he and Tug were worming their way into the narrow "bull's face," at the end of the easy pulling. They eased amid the stumps that represented the eyes and nostrils of "Taurus." From here they had to make an S-curve to get out past the nose and around the jaw stumps, and in doing that they'd also have to go up a little rise. Here Tug's great size and strength became especially important. He had to keep the sled turning but moving steadily. If he let its weight hold him to a stop, and then jerked it into an uphill start, he might yank the tongue apart. Without the slightest hesitation, Tug started into the S. . . .

Very soon after Tug had come, three years ago, they'd learned how strong and expert and calm about this business he was. In fact so expert and calm that Arley, who then had been eleven, had quickly learned to drive him alone. That meant Dad was free to work the chain saw, and Mom could drive the truck when it was loaded; and the work could go a lot faster.

So Arley and Tug had been working together now for three years, through the summers, and the weekends when school was on. Arley was almost always waking up or coming home to work that needed doing, and that work was almost always with Tug. Since he had no brothers or sisters, Tug had become as close a friend as he had. They didn't use many words, but Tug could say a lot in the way he twitched his ears or looked around with his huge long face; and Arley would speak with a few wordless sounds sometimes and by the way he wriggled the reins.

Now they were beginning the second curve of the S. They were almost past the "bull's jaw" and starting up the short but steep hump of the rise. One of Tug's big hooves pushed down on a branch that had been trimmed off one of the trees that had been cut there. The sharp end of the branch tipped up straight and jabbed him in the belly. Some horses would have spooked and become dangerous to handle over that, but Tug just kept smoothly leaning into the harness. And where a regular-sized tractor would have spun on the wet, moldy soil and maybe punctured its wide, costly tires on a stump, Tug just steadily shifted a little sideways so the sled would follow the same curve it always did. He had pulled it free of the "Taurus" stumps, and there was now a quarter of a mile left to go to the road.

At the top of the short rise, Arley reined Tug to a stop so they could both catch their breath. Behind them the chain saw had begun making short growls, which meant another tree was down and Dad was trimming off the limbs. Arley noticed the crows, which had made only a short flight, fly up out of the woods, disturbed again and cawing.

Now Arley really wanted to do some crowing, too. "Taurus" was one of the toughest stump passages they'd met in their three years of cutting and

clearing, and they'd made their way through it perfectly again. Arley wanted to jump and cheer, the
way he did in ball games at school when his team
made a big point.

He remembered the unfamiliar farm truck he'd
just seen going slowly past, and he guessed the people in it had been saying, "Look—there's someone
still logging with a horse. And *look* how they're
getting that load through all those stumps. That's
something!"

He remembered how Dad used to stand back
and exclaim: "Those two—Arley and Tug! They
could sneak a telephone pole through a picket
fence!"

But neither Dad or Mom remarked much about
how good he and Tug were anymore. The logs they
hauled were soon trucked away out of sight, and
the money from the logs was banked somewhere,
ready to buy new cows, as soon as there was money
and time enough to put up the new fencing they
would need. It seemed that Mom and Dad were
more interested in the future than in the present.

"We ought to celebrate how good we're doing
getting there," Arley thought.

He was resting by leaning with his hips against
the load of logs. He looked up at Tug's big sweat-
stained rump and then around at all the acres of
pulp wood they'd cleared for pasture. The deep

ground and tall sky and the wide forests around them seemed to soak up and muffle all the excitement he wanted to feel. Because the earth and sky were so large, and had had millions of years of changes, with probably millions of years more to come, it didn't matter to them that he and Tug spent a few days or a few years pulling logs for a few hundred yards. At the same time, he kept thinking about how much fun ballplayers had jumping and cheering each time they made a big point, and then they could enjoy it double by reading in the paper how well they played. He didn't want to have to wait quietly for applause the way the Earth could wait.

Arley stood straight up again. No point in thinking about what he couldn't produce. He looped the reins onto a corner of the log load and walked forward. He couldn't reach as high as Tug's ears, so he rubbed a fist lightly against the horse's neck. "Just look how we got through that bull's face again," he said quietly. Then his words started coming stronger and quicker: "You do more for us than any critter we've ever had. All by yourself. You ought to get more fun out of it than just doing it over and over. All you get are growls from a chain saw and a few caws from a bunch of crows—"

Arley paused, listening to the sound of his own words, flocking out of him like crows when they broke cover from among the trees. He tried some more: "And I know something *else* we could do," he said enthusiastically to Tug. "But we've got to start *soon*. You deserve it. And it'd be *special*. You know, there's lots of county fairs. But we can give the Feast Lake fair something no other fair's ever had! So it'd be special for *everybody*." For once, words seemed to be just rushing to his tongue to be said.

He'd already tried telling Mom and Dad and some friends at 4-H about his idea. They'd all smiled as if it were some passing joke. Arley decided he wasn't going to let it pass any more.

"Tonight," he told Tug, "I'm going to tell 'em just like I'm telling you. I've got the words now. I'll betcha I'll make 'em see I'm right."

First, of course, there was work to finish. Arley went back behind the load and took up the reins again. But before he could flick them to signal Tug to resume hauling, his thoughts were completely interrupted. Tug gave a brisk whistling kind of snort and shifted his whole body to the side with his head way high. Right then Arley saw a moving black shape—a bear had come out of the woods and was bounding toward them.

3

The Spies

WHEN THE SLOW-MOVING truck had gone a little way past the stumpy clearing and into a canyonlike opening where the county road led on through thick forest, it had moved to the side and stopped along the shady edge of the road, just before it reached a gray cement bridge over a weedy stream. The driver had gotten out and quietly lifted the truck's hood.

He was nineteen, stoutly and strongly built, with pale hair that was still pressed down from the bright yellow cap he'd left lying in the cab. He had stepped next around to the right hand door and said to his sister, who was still sitting inside, "I hope those crows don't keep fussing about us. If anyone comes by, just tell them the radiator boiled over and

I've gone for water."

"If I'm not here, I won't have to tell anyone anything," she'd replied. "They'll just guess from the hood being up. I want to come with you."

He'd hesitated just a second, then agreed. "Okay. But be quiet."

Then he'd gotten a plastic bucket from the truck's bed, and they'd slipped softly into the woods. They were able to move making only the gentlest sounds, for it had been a strange summer. There'd been hardly any good rains at all, so hay and other farm crops were going to be scarce and expensive. But there had been frequent light drizzles, just enough to dampen the woods, where the shade kept the dampness from evaporating and kept the fire danger low. Therefore, logging operations were able to continue.

At first they went along the creek because the cranberry bushes growing there were thin and tall and they could move among them easily. Then soon the brother said, "Well, we'd better get to where we can see that horse." And they turned to start making their way through the thick woods toward the clearing. At that moment the crows made their second flapping commotion above them, and in the next moment a bear, who had bedded down for the day close to his cranberries, despite the nearness of the road and the chain saw, heaved onto his feet in alarm. The brother and sister instantly stood more rigid than any tree around them, really more startled than scared, because it was just a black bear. The bear's first thought was of escape, and it plunged off through the woods, loudly batting any small saplings or brush in its way. It burst outward into the stump field, and by then the brother and sister were dashing after it to see what would happen.

The sister was sixteen, with broad shoulders for a girl, and she could move through the thick woods as athletically as her heavier brother. They reached the edge of the stump field together, and what they saw was—practically nothing. There was the bounding shape of the bear, going over the stumps and then disappearing into the woods at the other side of the clearing. The big horse and the boy were just standing watching.

"Look at that!" the brother exclaimed with a low hissing sound. "Most any horse would've kicked loose and run crazy if a bear came charging that close! What I heard about that horse was right. What luck to get proof, huh? That's the horse we want."

"You wouldn't want to take a good horse like that on your job," the girl objected.

"It's *our* job," the boy insisted quietly. "And we need the best we can get. We'll come get him in a couple weeks, the first night of the fair."

4

An Evening for Three

THAT EVENING IN HIS BARN, which had been sprayed and swept clean to keep down the annoyance of flies, Tug munched away at his grain. Later, in the cooler darkness, he'd go out and graze where a special two-wire fence had been put up for him around an area of stumps. He had seen bears before that afternoon, and none of them had ever been half as big as he was, so he'd never learned to be afraid of them, either in the daylight or in the dark.

If there had been other horses around, he would have been a little more active, jostling them for the biggest share of the grain, then joining them to graze or to stand cooperatively in a bunch swatting each other's flies. He had lived amid big bands of horses, and he'd lived alone like this. Tug could adjust. Either way there'd always been plenty of stray sounds to tickle his flickering ears and passing scents to interest his big wide nose. He didn't get excited in a herd, or mope when alone. He had no great ambitions and no sad memories and no pressing worries. He lived with what he had, and enjoyed every munch of every biteful.

THAT EVENING in the dining room, Arley was not so content. There were only two weeks till fair time, so he was arguing urgently for the idea he'd only mentioned hopefully the month before. "I've *already* asked Gene Carr about it at 4-H," he reported. "He's the one who'll be in charge at the fair. He says there's people that keep teams just to use at contests to see how much they can pull. But no one's ever figured how to show how *smart* a timber horse can be. This'll be different. People ought to know how good a horse Tug is. And will they be surprised!"

Mom saw it differently. "It seems just a bit braggy to me," she said. "And I'm sure it doesn't matter to Tug if he ever gets to a fair or has a ribbon tacked up and gathering dust in his barn. I'll bet that an extra bucket of grain and an extra day's rest is the kind of award Tug likes."

"He'd only need to put on one or two shows at the fair, so he'd get rest there," Arley put in. "Anyway," he added honestly, "I'm not sure he likes to rest a lot. And it'll be fun for *everybody*."

"It'd take a bit of extra work, and *time*, on our part, getting him there and getting a show with fifty tar buckets practiced and set up." Dad had said that once before, and he repeated it now. But gradually he came around to Arley's view. "You know," he said, "it just might not hurt to show people that even if we did have trouble on the plains, we still know how to handle livestock. That might make them more interested in buying our calves when we're ready to sell some."

"Okay." Mom gave in, in the end. "It's two against one. Arley and Tug will have a day at the fair."

THIRTY MILES AWAY, on the other side of Feast Lake and closer to the smaller town of Rune, the brother and sister were hurrying to finish the evening milking before dark. They were late because of their trip in the truck. They'd told their father and mother the trip was to look at some hay that was for sale, and that was partially true: they had gone to look at hay, after seeing the horse.

"You still going to tell him it was a year old and ninety-five dollars a ton?" the brother said as they finally started for the house. "We can't make any money feeding livestock at that price, and he'll know it."

"He also knows the weather's been too dry for crops, so the price'll be high," she insisted. "He'll only worry worse if we try to fool him."

As they climbed the back steps and opened the kitchen door, they heard faintly, from three miles away, the blaring horn of the evening freight train, bound toward Canada and blowing for its crossing with the road that ran past their place.

"Late as the freight," their mother said, as she'd said for years whenever the farmwork made supper late. Her words were as familiar and homey as the kitchen itself, but tonight there wasn't much spirit in them. And their father, again, did not come to the table. Some meals he did, and some meals he didn't. He'd suffered a stroke that had left him partially paralyzed. It was difficult for him to get around; and often after he'd tried to get around the farm anyway, he was exhausted and depressed. He could no longer contribute any work.

"I can't stand this any longer," their mother murmured as they ate. "Whatever it takes, we're going to send him down to Minneapolis for that program."

But there was nothing wrong with their father's ears.

"No, you're not!" he called from the other room, in a bellow that was mostly a squawk. "We've mortgaged all we can to pay for my heart as it is. We'd have to sell out for me to take six months treatment more, and I'm not robbing these kids for that. I'll get along as I am."

The next morning, as they started out to work, the sister whispered to her brother, "Mom's right! He's getting worse. Every *one* of those doctors said if he doesn't start soon, it won't work. I can't stand letting him cripple around here any more."

"Just hang in a couple weeks," the brother said, under his breath, "and I'll have the cash we need for it."

By then they were past a leafy hedge that grew around the edge of the yard, taller than they were. They couldn't be seen from the house. The sister spun around in front of her brother, forcing him to halt a moment. Her cheeks were wide like his, and though her skin was smoother, her pale blue eyes were just as firm. "And I can't stand what you're planning, either." She kept her voice quiet, but it practically sizzled. "You know what'll happen if you get caught. Dad'll have such a shock it'll finish him."

"*Listen.*" The brother glowered at her. "Do you *want* to lose this farm, just because some bad luck gangs up on us all in one year?"

"Of course not."

As she answered, he sidestepped around her and went on walking. From the side of his mouth he said, "And you do want Pop to have that therapy that'll maybe get him moving?"

"*Yes*," she said as she kept pace beside him. "Pop needs it *now*. So we'll have to sell this place now. That's the price we'll have to pay."

"No. It's not!" he said fiercely as they went into the overnight lot to move the cows into the milking shed. It was attached to the big barn, where most of their cattle spent the snowy winters indoors. When the milking was done and the cows turned out, the two went into the toolroom part of the barn where he lifted a coil of wire off a peg and began rummaging in cans of old bolts and nails, while she got a saw and augur drill and two wrenches and a couple hammers and put them into a wooden carrying box. One of their gate posts had become rotten with age and needed fixing before the cows pushed it down and wandered along the road in their search for fresh grass. "With this deal I've made"—the brother finally spoke again, as they started to leave—"we'll swing the doctors and that mortgage both. Because we'll get enough money quick enough."

"Gregg," she hissed, "if you go to jail for smuggling and stealing, we'll have to sell anyway, and it *will* kill Dad. To say nothing of purposely killing a horse. I get sick when I even think of that."

The brother didn't answer till they'd loaded their tools and wire and a post they'd cut the day before and started driving the truck to the gate. "Because I think of it, don't mean I like it," he said angrily, his voice louder than the rumbling sounds inside the cab. "Even though I didn't make this problem, I got to solve it. And I'd rather try to have both this place and his treatment than just give in. So I *am* going to make a try for it," he said, and she saw him turn to glare those words directly into her. Then, when they came to the gate, he shut off the motor and in the silence looked at her again. He spoke quieter, but just as fiercely. "If you get in the way," he told her, as he'd told her before, "there's a double chance I will get caught. And that means you, too. If you'll help, it's an almost sure thing we'll make it. It's just a one-shot deal, in and out in one night, and we're home free, with six thousand bucks to pay our way. You were smart enough to overhear what I arranged and get yourself mixed in. Now be smart enough not to jam it up. There won't be another chance like this."

The girl held her breath, thinking. She wasn't big enough to knock him down and pound some sense into him, and she was scared of what else he might try to do if she got in his way. She would have to go along at least until fair time, so she would keep knowing what he was up to. At the same time she'd try to find some way to stop him without letting Pop know about it, for Pop would get too excited trying to stop it himself.

"Okay," she agreed quietly. But then she sat up straighter and told him, fiercely, herself, "But *you* keep being smart and quiet about it, too!"

They sat staring back aand forth, until their anger with each other burned down, and together they went to fix the gate.

TWO

To the Fair
and Gone

5

Tug on the Town

THE FIRST DAY OF AUGUST
was the first day of the Timber County Fair, and
Tug arrived in town early, traveling alone in a horse
trailer that was built to carry two horses. He backed
out of it onto the playground of the Feast Lake
Grade School, where a number of other horses were
also gathering. There were neatly groomed and sleek
saddle horses, which seemed to turn almost scrawny
and practically disappear when they walked close
by and the morning sun threw Tug's shadow completely over them. There were ponies, including a
half-dozen all decorated with the same-colored rig-
ging, that could've walked right under Tug. There
were also big horses, team horses, though none of

them was as tall or stretchy as Tug. Some of those teams were hitched just to empty traces, while others were pulling light gigs full of people dressed in old-fashioned top hats, sunbonnets, long dresses and knee-length knicker pants.

Tug's ears sampled all the sounds, but he turned his head only slowly to look at another horse throwing a fuss or at a squeaky wagon going by. He looked around with more interest as the familiar man and boy put a saddle onto his back and tightened it around his ribs with extra long latigo straps. It had been years since Tug had carried a saddle, so even though he'd just had a week of short practice sessions and was now used to it, he still regarded the thing as a bit curious.

Then a man's voice sounded, strange and loud, through a bullhorn megaphone, and the boy was boosted up onto the saddle, and all the horses began to move toward the playground gate. At the boy's urging, Tug began a slow, heavy-footed trot till he was in front of them all. He was in his first full dress parade, and already he'd been chosen to lead a section of it, for he was clearly the tallest animal there.

As he passed through the gate onto Eighth Street, he found himself next to a line of trucks with bright papier-mâché floats on them. Tug could not understand these nor the line of old machinery muttering away and squeezing off short blasts of steam whistles. Some of the other horses swung about sideways in nervousness, but Tug was just curious. Then one band began to play, and then another; several men in the street began waving short paddles, giving directions, and the different parts of the parade began to move, taking turns getting into positions in the center of the street, so that although he was in front of the horses, Tug gradually found himself in the middle of a long procession that marched and rolled and whistled and drummed and trumpeted five blocks up Eighth Street, then turned east, into the sun, onto Loggers Lane, which was a street that some finicky townspeople were always trying to get renamed "Main" or "Central" or something more "dignified."

Tug wasn't concerned much about what things were called, or about all the sounds that had become more or less steady, or even about all the crowds of people along the curbs or the dogs and bicycles that darted or swooped near him. Yet his feet were lifting jerkily, and he kept moving his big head to look behind, as if he'd left something behind he wanted to go back for. He knew he wasn't going idly back to the barn, that he was at *some* kind of work, and it felt unfamiliar—and therefore uncomfortable—to be working without hauling a load behind him. The hundred-fifty pounds of boy and saddle on his back were little compared to his own eighteen hundred pounds; and besides, he could tell —by the boy's touch on the reins and the scent of the boy's perspiration that came down to him—that the boy was nervous, and that was not usual.

Just the same, Tug kept on stepping. Life, as Tug had learned it from a calm mother and kind owners, was basically a matter of putting one foot in front of the other. Some steps were harder to make, or wetter or colder or noisier than others; but once you made enough of them, there were sure to be good things, like food and rest, waiting.

So by the corner of Ninth and Loggers Lane, Tug was getting himself used to being in a parade, and was marching along quite smoothly.

He had no reason to worry about the stout, strong young man who stood on the corner of Tenth and Loggers Lane, even though Tug noticed that under the bright yellow cap, which had caught his attention, the man seemed to watch him very closely as he stepped by.

6

Everybody Gets Ready

RIDING ON TOP OF TUG, Arley felt as if he were steering down the street on a steamboat. He'd never before seen a parade from such a high, central position. It felt good to be above the crowd and to be noticed, as long as he could feel that people were impressed by what they saw. And it seemed certain by the way some of them pointed and some of them turned their heads, that they were amazed that such a horse lived in their area. He could imagine them talking about looking for *that horse* later on inside the fairgrounds and wondering if such a horse might be there to *do* anything.

Arley almost grinned, thinking how surprised and impressed they were yet to be. And why not? It wasn't braggy. If he and Tug could do something so well, why not have fun showing it off and letting other people enjoy watching?

Yet—Arley began to imagine what it would be like if all those people stopped being amazed or impressed, if they started laughing at you, or scoffing, or just shook their heads and turned away, bored. After all, no one had begged him to be in the fair. He *had* bragged a bit to get a place on the program. And working in front of a staring crowd was bound to be different from being out with the woods and crows. Even if Tug had worked perfectly and intelligently at home for three years, if he got confused today, or stumbled on unfamiliar ground, who'd believe what he'd done before?

Arley hadn't worried about getting nervous. He hadn't even thought about getting nervous, but now he felt stage fright creeping up on him. So before they even reached Tenth Street and Loggers Lane, he quit watching the crowd. He just paid attention to the sounds of the music and looked only at the parade that he could see stretched out in front of him —until gradually the parade wound into the fairgrounds at the edge of town and was over.

The marchers began separating. Arley rode Tug to the fair's horse barn and got him unsaddled and stalled and fed and watered. Usually he paused a few moments to watch the contented way Tug ate. There was a lot of satisfaction in giving a creature that big something he enjoyed but couldn't get for himself.

This time Arley just tossed in the hay and ran off to the southeast part of the grounds to be sure the poles and empty tar buckets he and Dad had delivered two days ago were still there. The poles lay in a row, just as they'd put them, and the buckets were sitting upright, scattered about an area with a single-wire fence around it. At a corner of that fence, a colorful sign he'd painted still announced:

Special Surprise Performance
Team Pulling Area
Friday, 3 P.M.

He also jogged about making sure the four other signs that he'd put up around the fair were still in position. Then he found Gene Carr, the 4-H leader who'd be in charge of the team-pulling area, to be sure he was ready for them. Gene Carr was in charge of several other areas as well and said only, "Sure, you betcha," in a cheerful but hurried and impersonal way. It made Arley feel that though he'd been living around the town of Feast Lake for three years, he was still pretty much a stranger and would be all on his own that afternoon.

His parents wouldn't be there for two reasons. First, the pulp mill liked to keep its machinery going steadily and so sometimes would only buy from people who contracted to give them a steady supply of wood. It had already taken some time away from their logging to get Tug practiced for the fair, so Dad and Mom had gone back home to cut more logs and haul some that were already piled and were due at the mill on their contract. Secondly, Mom had suggested that since Arley had no brothers or sisters and had been home alone most of the summer, it would be good for him to be on his own with the other kids who'd be at the fair. "If he can't take care of Tug and keep out of trouble on his own, then we'd better know it now," she'd said, and Dad had agreed. Arley had not objected.

Now he was hurrying back to the horse barn to make sure he hadn't done anything wrong in his hurry before and to get ready for the afternoon. As he cut inward around the corner of the barn's main opening, he collided with someone just leaving. Arley was a little embarrassed because it was his fault for coming too recklessly, so he didn't look at the guy very well, except to see that he was stout and his body was hard. His face under a bright yellow cap wasn't too old.

"*Oof—* Sorry!" Arley offered.

"Sorry." The guy nodded and went on, and Arley forgot him. He checked on Tug; everything seemed okay. Then he went to the north end of the barn, to the open square room with a wooden floor raised like a stage, where people who were showing animals could spread out bedrolls and stay near them even at night. He planned to stay at least one extra day at the fair in case anyone wanted to see Tug perform again.

Dad and Mom had delivered his sleeping bag, clothes kit and the harness sack there during the parade. Arley found his equipment, pulled the heavy harness leathers free and began straightening them out, ready to be buckled on. By then it was nearly one o'clock, and he realized he was hungry. He knew from experience that he'd do better at three o'clock if his stomach didn't have a hollow ache, so he stood up to go out for a couple of quick hot dogs or something—and he noticed a girl standing by Tug's stall.

She wasn't fat or squat or ugly in any way, but she seemed like she'd be strong. She had broad shoulders for a girl. Then suddenly she turned to look his way, and her face was strangely pretty. Pretty because all her features had soft, thin edges. Strange because she looked familiar; he felt he ought to know her from somewhere, and for an instant thought about calling to her, but couldn't think of any name.

Just as abruptly she turned away and began moving toward the outside doorway. The way she'd turned made Arley feel a little embarrassed again, as if he'd been caught staring when he shouldn't have been. But he knew he hadn't been rude and decided his nervousness was making him edgy. So he forgot about her and went off, trying to think just about two hot dogs, with mustard and pickle relish, plus something for dessert.

7

Tug Among the Tar Buckets

Early that afternoon Tug found himself being "dressed" in his harness straps and loose fly netting. Then he led the way out of the barn into the sunshine, with the boy walking behind him and guiding him by the long reins.

There were more people on the fairgrounds than Tug had seen when he'd gone into the barn, and he had to step slowly among them. There were strange smells coming from some of the buildings he passed and especially from the cotton candy stalls. The gaudy metal frameworks of the carnival rides were odd things to him. There were so many unfamiliar things, in addition to the unusual nervousness he could still feel in the way the boy handled the reins, that Tug was puzzled, and extra alert. But since he could not sense anything to really become alarmed about, he remained calm.

They came to a place where other horses were already gathered, all of them in teams of two. Some of the teams were shaking busily against flies and stomping restlessly. Some had netting to help them, and some did not. Other teams were covered with sweaty foam and were too spent to fuss much for a while. These had just had their turns straining against sleds full of cement weights, to see which team could move the heaviest load.

Tug moved around the teams and the people who were watching them, and then, still obeying the light directions of the reins, he stopped beside a single-wire fence, next to three long logs and near to some scattered tar buckets that he immediately recognized. He was also close to a sign announcing:

Special Surprise Performance
Team Pulling Area
Friday, 3 P.M.

Tug didn't understand what was on the sign, or why the boy didn't hitch him right away to a log so they could get started working. But since he got no more directions, he simply stood waiting. From behind him, he heard grunts and shouts and smelled dust and sweat, as more horse teams strained to move the cement weights. Every once in a while some clapping sounds or a human voice strangely loud as it echoed through a bullhorn megaphone roused him out of a doze.

Tug didn't understand what the man with the bullhorn announced when three o'clock came, and he didn't particularly stir when the group of people shifted to gather around him. But when he saw that one of the logs was being attached to his harness, Tug woke up immediately. And when the boy—with very nervous pulls—loosened the fence wire so it fell, and then reined him toward the tar buckets, Tug knew just what to do, because he and the boy had been pulling logs through stands of tar buckets several times a day for the past few days, out by the barn in the woods. Tug didn't know that those had been just practice sessions and this was the "real thing." He just saw another job to be done and started to do it.

He didn't consider that tar buckets could be knocked askew much easier than rooted stumps. He didn't worry that he might be laughed at or jeered at, or left behind if people got bored. He'd always had men around him when he'd worked in the larger lumber camps, so the watching faces didn't really bother him. What distracted most was the boy's nervousness, which he felt in the reins; but since that had been going on most of the day, Tug was starting to get used to that, too. Guided by the reins' nervous wrigglings, he dug in his big hooves—and steadily, pausing only briefly whenever he had to back or shift to the side to start a turn, he easily pulled that single log on a twisting trail among the maze of stumplike tar buckets, and out the far end, without tipping or even touching a one.

The people behind him made the clapping sounds again. Tug didn't understand why, but it didn't bother him either. The boy—handling the reins a lot less nervously—directed him in a circle around toward where they'd begun. On their way they passed the man with the yellow cap among the other staring eyes. Because he'd noticed that man from the parade and had seen him close in the barn, Tug recognized him as someone familiar among strangers, but that was no reason to interrupt what he was doing. A second log was hooked on, and Tug hauled the two among the buckets as expertly as the first.

Again the people clapped their hands.

Next Tug went back past the yellow-cap-man for the third log and pulled it through, and by then the boy's touch on the reins had become as smooth and confident as it had grown to be in the woods. And the people clapped very loudly, but that noise still didn't bother Tug any.

Then the boy, in a very peppy and cheerful

manner, directed him back to the barn and gave him fresh feed and water, along with a thorough curry-combing and rubdown.

Old Tug figured he'd had an easy day.

8

The Tap After Train Time

As Tug munched contentedly, Arley went off to see the rest of the fair. He walked out of the barn into the late afternoon coolness, feeling as tall as he'd felt in the saddle during the parade.

He and Tug had put on *some* performance! He'd known from the clappings and murmurings that the people watching had been amazed and entertained. Maybe now others would try it. "Log Steering," they might call it. Or they might call it "Tug's Game," when they realized how much skill it took: not just muscle but brains too, and no whips cracking, but friendship between you and your horse. He was sure no one could ever do it better than Tug and he.

As Arley inspected the other exhibits—from brightly sewn quilts to smoothly brushed hogs—they all seemed very interesting and worth a first prize, because his own exhibit had gone so well. Then for a while he had double the usual fun tossing baseballs and rings for prizes, because he could relax and not worry about seeming clumsy. He'd already proved he was an expert at something. He wished Mom and Dad had come to watch. And he kept waiting, hoping for someone to come up to him to talk more about it, ask him how he'd managed the practicing, if he and Tug would perform again, maybe as a paid act somewhere. In the morning he'd been nervous about what would happen. Now he was so busy celebrating that at first he didn't hear the man who spoke to him, not till the repeated words broke into his thoughts like hail through a glass window.

"That horse sure knows his stuff, don't he?" a tall, rather flat-faced man was saying. It was Jeff Raybel, their neighbor.

Suzette, his wife, was beside him, with her usually loose gray hair now bound in tight waves close about her head. "You handled him as good as any man we've ever hired," she added.

"We get along real good," Arley answered.

And a little later, as he was giving a close eye to the prize pies, a wiry man, who was also looking hungrily at them, recognized him. He had a kind of odd name, Ben Crease; Arley remembered it because he'd seen the man at the pulp mill office.

"Say, I saw that show you put on this afternoon." Ben Crease grinned. "You must be a pretty good horse trainer."

"Tug likes to work," Arley replied. "We do it every day at home."

"Why, maybe you ought to sell tickets and hold shows while you get some real work done."

"Hey, I'll ask Dad about that." Arley laughed, yet for a moment he also thought about it seriously. He was just deciding that the suggestion was a friendly joke when a few kids he knew from school spoke to him, but about nothing in particular. They were just pausing on their way to the rides and asked him to come along. But Arley didn't feel in the mood for an aimless kind of evening right then. Suddenly he was wondering if there were other, more usable ideas that he ought to be thinking of and working on. Maybe Tug didn't care if he was applauded for all the special skill he had and didn't care about getting to do something different once in a while, but maybe he did care! And he sure deserved it. Then, too, as Dad said, if people knew how good they were with animals, they'd be more interested in buying their calves.

So, made hungry again by the pies, Arley bought himself a sandwich-and-pop supper and sat eating it thoughtfully as the last of the afternoon dimmed slowly into evening. The colored lights from the carnival part of the fair glittered more brightly as the sky darkened. From close by, the blare of a diesel horn cut through his thoughts, then he heard a low rumble moving onto the main tracks past the fairgrounds. He listened to the heavy rhythm of the train moving on toward Canada, and toward tomorrow.

Tomorrow, Arley thought, maybe someone else'll think of where Tug might put on a show and come to find him. Now that people knew what Tug could do, tomorrow might be a day for ideas. Arley decided to spend the last of his day's allowance on a double ice cream and go to bed early. He'd been awake since dawn and wanted to be alert in the morning. He bussed his tray to the trash barrel and counter. Then he felt a tap on his shoulder.

A pleasant voice said, "Excuse me. Aren't you the boy who has the big horse who could pull logs so neatly?"

Arley gave her a smile and a happy, "Yes!"— and realized he was looking at the same pretty girl he'd seen standing by Tug's stall at noon. Her eyes kind of glistened above wide cheekbones, and she had a smooth, fine jaw making a kind of dipping curve below smiling lips. Again he felt there was something familiar about her face, yet he still couldn't decide why.

"He's got to be the strongest, cleverest horse around," she said.

"I sure think so," he agreed. Mom had warned him not to talk braggy, but he thought that was a good, honest reply. It was confidence, not brag.

"He seemed so calm, despite having to work in a crowd," the girl said. "I bet he could learn quickly to do a lot of things."

"We'd sure be willing to try," Arley told her, and he felt his pulse starting to move faster at the thought of an opportunity that might be coming.

"Has anyone asked about renting him, or buying him? Today, I mean."

"Well—" Arley didn't want to admit that no one had been that enthusiastic. "I've been moving around quite a bit. Anyway, I wouldn't want to sell him."

"How long since you've seen him?" the girl asked in an abrupt way.

"Oh, not since we performed and I curried him down," Arley answered. "Like I said, I've been busy looking aroun—"

The girl startled him by grasping his arm. "Let's go look at him now," she said, and her voice suddenly seemed to spark with impatience.

Taken by surprise, Arley automatically pulled back. "Well, wait, I—"

"Please," she said, with excitement. "I'd like to meet him, and I don't have much time."

"But—" Arley didn't like to be yanked around. "Weren't you in the barn this noon?"

"That's not the same!" she exclaimed. "Standing there like a stranger. I want to be introduced by someone who's his friend. Come, please, can't you go with me now?"

That was more than Arley could resist. Her excitement seemed odd, but not confused or silly. She seemed serious and urgent, and she understood that he was friends with Tug, not just an owner.

She was maybe two years older than he was, and her grip was about as strong and rough as a man's, but he felt good running hand-in-hand with her. It was probably going to be fun introducing her to Tug and talking about horses with her. Maybe she knew people who'd be interested in seeing what Tug and he could do. He'd have to keep her from running off again too quickly.

He made her slow up a little as they got near the barn door, and they entered without bumping into anyone. The inside of the barn was gloomy.

The few light bulbs were all small and high up on the rafters, and as he glanced around, Arley got just a glimpse of some kids and older people setting out bedrolls in the sleeping room, and he vaguely noticed three people in the aisles and stalls taking care of other horses. But he couldn't see Tug's head above his stall, and when he got to that stall he saw nothing but wood and a water bucket and scattered hay.

He stood and blinked and stared.

There was old worn wood and a half-empty water bucket made of strong green plastic and a half-empty bunk of hay. And some dark droppings. But no horse. Tug was gone.

9

The Truck Bed Battle

At that moment Tug was fifteen miles away, looking down over the back edge of the truck on which he'd been riding along a dusty road through the dim gray twilight. The truck had come to a stop in murkier darkness beneath the trees at the edge of a forest, and now the stout young man in the yellow cap was pulling on the rope attached to Tug's halter, trying to get him to jump off.

Tug held back. He had been traveling tied face-to-the-front with the wind of travel batting him in the face. His eyes were full of dust and tear moisture so he couldn't see well. The man was invisible to him in that blurred darkness. The yellow cap was just a pale shape, like an angry bird moving jerkily about in midair.

It wasn't the "bird" that was bothering Tug. He'd never been attacked by a bird and was too big and calm to let such a thing bother him now. Besides that, everything smelled perfectly normal for a forest. But he couldn't tell if the ground below him was smooth or dangerous with knobby roots. He knew that if he jumped, his great weight would strike down just on the old joints of his front legs. Instinct warned him not to take the risk.

Yellow Cap's voice began to encourage him in gruff whispers. "Hyah. C'mon. Get off!"

Tug still hesitated.

When Yellow Cap had come to the stall at the fair barn and had quickly haltered him and led him out, Tug had accepted that. No one had ever given him advance notice of such changes. He'd followed the pull of the rope away from the busy noises and lights, over by the railroad tracks, and into some pens that had loading chutes for trucks as well. He'd grown used to getting on strange trucks at different places, and he'd ridden patiently, despite the headwind. Tug had been moving, or stopping, at men's commands for so long that he'd almost forgotten how to resist. But that dark drop-off now at the back of the truck was reminding him.

Yellow Cap began yanking harder at the halter

rope. The man's voice kept whispering, but became sharper with anger, which made Tug even less eager to go closer to him and to the edge. Then Tug began to scent, from the man's sweat, something more disturbing than the anger, and worse than the nervousness he'd detected in the boy earlier. It was the scent of fear. Yet Yellow Cap kept yanking hard. He was strong.

But Tug was much stronger.

Still holding the rope, Yellow Cap picked up a long piece of dead branch, came alongside the truck, and began poking at Tug through the wooden slats.

Tug felt the branch tip jab into his stomach and hips and tried to get away from the pain of it; but he had very little room to move on the truck bed, which rocked spookily as he shifted about. The man's voice, still not loud, kept snarling at him. The scent of fear stayed thick. Then quite by accident Tug's hip jammed the dead branch against the side of the truck, and something split with a tearing screech. For a moment Yellow Cap's voice got loud and very fierce-sounding.

But the jabbing pains in Tug's hip and stomach stopped, and he would not be frightened by merely a voice into jumping blindly.

The man stomped around to face Tug again from the back of the truck, and there—much more softly—he coaxed at Tug, until he got him to at least put his head in front of the truck's back opening. Then right away Yellow Cap stretched out the halter rope and wrapped the other end quickly around a tree and tied it. After which he went and got into the truck's cab.

Tug heard the motor start, and the truck began to move slowly away from the tree. The pull of the rope and halter against Tug's head got taut, then extremely strong.

Really stirred to resisting now, Tug pulled hard against it. If the rope broke he would tumble dangerously backward in the truck. But his hoofs could get no good grip on the slippery truck bed. With the halter and rope holding his head, and the truck moving away beneath him, his feet skidded to the truck's back edge, and he had to flounder off, out through the narrow opening in a desperate scrambling jump in which he lifted himself just high enough that his hind legs had an extra instant to stretch down and reach the ground at *almost* the same time as his front legs. The ground was smooth, and the soil soft and cushiony, but the grip of the rope held his head too low, so that he over-balanced into the start of a forward tumble that could have broken his neck. With his hind legs striking down, his old muscles had had enough exercise that by sheer strength he held himself upright. But his neck absorbed the terrible wrenching.

The truck paused with its motor still mumbling. Yellow Cap came back. He checked the halter fastenings and the knot at the tree.

"That got you off," he said triumphantly, though the smell of fear still lingered about him. "Now you just stay here till I get back."

Yellow Cap went again into the truck and drove away.

Tug hadn't understood the man's words. He was just glad to see him go. He tested the woods again and found that they still smelled and sounded peaceful and normal. So, since the fuss had made him hungry and thirsty again, he began to nose for whatever moist greenery there was to bite at—but pains in his stiffening neck made him do that slowly and a little awkwardly. He gave the rope no more fight. He just stood patiently eating whatever he could reach, as he'd done for years whenever he'd been tied. The fire of resistance that had flamed up from long ago when he'd been a young colt had faded out again.

10

To Shout or to Run?

STOP!" THE GIRL HAD
pushed her hand up against his mouth, whispering
hurriedly. "Don't *say anything*," she told him.

Arley shook her off. "Hey!" he called toward
the other people in the barn. "Did anyone see where
this horse went?"

Faces looked up at him from the aisles and
peered out from the sleeping room. No one could
see anyone else very well in the weak light from the
small bulbs high above, but the faces all slowly
shook. For a weird moment they all seemed to be
just like the mechanical dolls he'd seen at some of
the carnival booths, though he heard a chorus of
very real voices say, "No," and, "Nope," and, "Sure

didn't." One man said, "If he's got loose, I'll help you look in a minute."

The girl squeezed his arm, hard, and pulled him back around. There was no doubt that she was strong. "Don't *wait* for them," she hissed very urgently. "They don't know where your horse is. I do."

"You know?"

"Yes. C'mon. There's *no time*," she pleaded quietly, and pulled at him strongly to go back outside.

Arley, alarmed now and bewildered, started to go with her. "What's going on?" he demanded as he moved.

"Tell you later," she whispered. Then as they passed out the doorway with her still gripping his arm, she said, "Let's run!"

Arley dug in and made her stop. "Run where?"

She pulled to keep running. Overhead there was no longer any sky, just the airy gleam of the fair's lights from the other side of the barn; the various colors made her face glow like the ghost of a clown. "*Follow,*" she insisted as she kept hauling at him. She began having to speak between deep breaths. "You horse is stolen. You've got to get him back. Or they'll kill him when they're done!"

That gave Arley visions of a slaughterhouse and Tug secretly being brought there and weighed and sold by the pound for dog food. He yanked completely loose from her, saying, "We've got to get the cops!"

She sprang and grasped him again, stood close against him, her eyes looking directly into his. Her voice stayed quiet, but came at him as intensely as the crackling heat of a fire: "*No*," she commanded. "*There's no time*. If you yell for the cops, I won't help you. I won't tell you where he's gone. I won't even know you."

"Why?" he demanded. Again, especially with her face up close, he felt that he'd met her somewhere, though surely not in school. What did that have to do with Tug? "*Look*," he added, "if this is a ransom deal, we don't have any money."

Her eyes and mouth each squeezed together for an instant as if in pain. "It's *not* for ransom!" she exclaimed, though still quietly. "I'm trying to help you save your horse. Cops can't help. And if those people come out here and see me with you, I can't help. Honest, we've got to hurry *now!*" She was starting to plead again, no longer giving orders. "Please, believe me," she begged him. "Trust me. Please!"

There was just too much urgency about her, and mystery, and prettiness, for Arley to keep resisting. He remembered it was she who'd found him and hurried him to the barn to find Tug gone, earlier than he would've come, so she must know something. He was convinced that Tug was in danger and decided he didn't dare delay.

"All right," he agreed, "let's go," and right away he was following her at a run, along the dim and edges of the fairgrounds, past loading pens and onto the parking lot that spread out north of the fair, between the highway and the railroad tracks.

She stopped him beside a small motorcycle. "Okay," she breathed rapidly, "Get on."

"You old enough to drive this?"

"I can handle it. Get on." She was loosening a helmet locked by a tight strap to a handlebar.

"I don't have one of those," he said. "The cops'll stop us."

"I hope they're too busy. We won't go to the highway."

"Then where—?"

"I'll show. C'mon."

There seemed no point in arguing now. Arley got on the seat behind her. It was a small seat that forced him to press against her back, and he put one arm around her waist for balance. She started the cycle, and with its motor muttering softly, they began gliding among the parked cars and trucks, with the headlight off.

In the far corner of the parking lot they came to the bracing of its barbed wire fence. Built into that corner-bracing was an old gate of stiff wire and rusty pipe. Beyond the gate was the railroad track.

"We'll go along the tracks, a ways," she said. "No one'll bother us there."

"Suppose a train—"

"The northbound's gone. No more till after midnight."

Again there seemed no point in more arguing. Arley got off, untwisted the old wire holding the gate shut, and hefted it open, then together they shoved the cycle onto the railroad right-of-way, and he went back to close the gate.

The ride was every bit as bouncy as he'd figured it would be, rolling along over the wooden ties between the rails. But as long as they went slowly, they could go steadily and hang on. The woods that were soon thick and dark on both sides gave them only a narrow strip of starlight overhead by which to see what kind of bounce awaited them from moment to moment, since the girl had not turned the cycle's light on. It meant, Arley thought, that they weren't going to get very far.

Then, after about a mile, they passed a pale white post standing by the tracks to warn engineers of a road crossing. It turned out to be a country road of sandy gravel, and as the girl steered onto it she flicked on the headlight, twisted up the throttle, and they scooted onward at a faster, smoother, windier speed.

THREE

Into the Forest, to the Moon

11

Dark Sounds, Shapes, and Sloughs

EVEN IN EARLY AUGUST the northern nights were cool. It made the mosquitoes slow, but they had begun to discover Tug. He'd begun to hear their faint humming as they explored closer. Then, slightly louder, he'd begun hearing some occasional soft stirrings and snappings getting closer amid the thick brush that grew around the small opening in the forest where he was tied. Then he sniffed a faint aroma that he'd sniffed at other times, as a female porcupine came slowly foraging to the edge of the opening. Tug didn't turn his head toward her, for the movement would've increased the ache in his wrenched neck.

He had just had time to give her the calm curious attention of one eye, when the porcupine suddenly got a clear whiff of horse. It was a scent she had never met before. Tug heard her startled snort, and his one eye now watched more curiously as she peered about, till he saw her kind of spin back into the brush, disappearing with a quick scurrying that he heard go further and more softly away.

Next, as if called by the porcupine's snort, a stronger rattling began in the treetops. It didn't fade away or come closer. Instead, it stayed steadily above, as Tug stiffly looked up a little. His ears flickered, then stiffly but calmly he reached down for more grass. He might have wished the breeze that was springing up would come down through the woods to puff away the mosquitoes. But the treetops caught all the breeze and kept it aloft, passing it busily from leafy branch to leafy branch. Because of the wind-sounds overhead, Tug didn't hear the soft thumping of cautious footsteps until moments before Yellow Cap reappeared.

The man's broad back seemed hunched, for he was wearing a small knapsack. He was carrying two things that Tug immediately recognized: an axe and a lanky coil of rope.

"All right. Couldn't see anyone else around,"

Yellow Cap murmured, as if talking to Tug as well as himself.

Yellow Cap's voice was calm, yet Tug again sensed a hint of fear in the man's movements and odor. Tug still couldn't detect anything in the woods to be frightened of, but what he sensed about the man kept him alert.

Yellow Cap untied the thick halter rope from the tree. "Let's go," he muttered, and led off along a vague passageway among the trees. A lot of the windblown grit had drained out of Tug's eyes by now, into cakey stains on the hair of his cheeks. He could see better, and he needed to see better. The forest branches mingled over the top of the lane, and even though they were stirring in the new breeze, very little starlight was sneaking through. The tall grasses that had grown up in the lane looked dense in the darkness, but were really thin and lightly brushed away the mosquitoes as Tug stepped through them.

He followed Yellow Cap for about two miles, until his thirst began to tickle him worse as he smelled the sharp dampness of a slough. The water there would be dark but clear as it trickled through its channel of half-rotten grasses. When they reached it, it was a double slough: two long depressions with a narrow mossy-dry hummock running along between them. In the springtime both channels would be chest deep with icy water from melting snow and rain. In the winters they were full of snow, and the old-time loggers had made a frozen level trail right across them. But now, this summer, they held more mud than water, and Yellow Cap started slogging right through them, without giving Tug any chance to seek a puddle to drink.

The slogging was tough. Their feet sank deep, and they pulled them out only with strong effort and loud sucking slurps. There was treeless sky over the slough, full of stars that made the night air right there seem almost bright, compared to the darkness in the woods, while many mosquitoes rose up like a fog from underneath. Yellow Cap began spitting and blowing at the mosquitoes, because with one hand holding the halter rope and the other arm carrying the axe and rope coil, he couldn't do anything else to them. He had not put on any insect repellent for fear that if things went wrong and he needed to hide, the scent of it might give him away.

Old Tug snorted some too and swept his tail and vibrated all the muscles of his skin the handy way a horse can. He wanted to shake his mane also, but didn't because the soreness in his neck prevented him. So as soon as they were past the slough onto more trail, Tug lowered his head deep into the grasses to brush off the mosquitoes that had gathered around his eyes. That movement pulled Yellow Cap backward a little, and the man, not understanding, immediately jerked the halter rope forward, hissing, "C'mon, keep going." The strong jerk hurt Tug's neck so that he raised his head with some of the mosquitoes still riding.

He had to put up with them less than another mile before they came near the edge of a clearing that was large enough for the wind to be dipping down across it. The air filtering into the woods there was full of the smell of water. But Yellow Cap stopped and again tied Tug to a tree. The man hissed, "You stay here," then slowly crept away, bent over like a quietly prowling bear.

Tug brushed off the insects and calmly tested his new situation. He could sense nothing about more bothersome than the mosquitoes. Standing still, he could even hear the lapping of waves along a shore. But he couldn't get to them to drink, so he began munching leaves off the tree.

Once, the scent of the man came back to him in the air, but soundlessly, and then the scent faded, and he didn't smell it again till the man came quietly back to him from behind. "Okay, I've been all around. There's no one laying for us. Let's go," the man muttered.

He led Tug out into a broad clearing where there were many bright stars overhead and thick grass underfoot. Also, dark in the clearing were tall, angular shapes. Tug raised his head, alertly appraising them. Then as Yellow Cap jerked his head with the reins to keep him moving, Tug recognized that there were familiar smells and angles and spaces to those shapes. They were parts of an old sawmill camp.

This mill had been started in pioneer days, when the timber had been huge and had never before heard the ring of a steel axe. Those trees had all been cut and sawed and carried off more than sixty years before, and the land left to grow up again, into the kinds of woods—mostly smaller pulp-sized trees—that Tug knew. He'd worked at several of the newer mills that had also been built next to ponds or lakes, because the logs that were hauled in could be handled more easily in water. They were floated into position beside the ramps that lifted them up to meet the saws.

Tug could tell, with increasing thirsty eagerness, that there was a lake full of water just down past the line of trees at the other side of the clearing. But instead of leading him all the way to drink, Yellow Cap tied the halter rope to a rusting, half-buried heap of metal that had once been used to gouge sled-runner ruts in the old winter roads of ice. Then he disappeared behind the broken wall of a building.

Tug's thirst was annoying but not yet desperate. He'd never in his life become desperately thirsty. So he didn't pull at the halter rope, though he kept smelling the big water strongly and hearing the breeze-pushed waves ploshing against its shore. The dipping breeze was keeping away the mosquitoes. Patiently he eased his hurt neck downward and began enjoying all the grass he could reach.

12

Roadside Stand

THE GIRL DRIVING THE
motorcycle was practically in Arley's lap as he clung
to her from the back part of the seat. But there
wasn't much chance to talk, for she kept her helmet
on and steered as fast as she could. Every so often
they would come to a road and she would turn.
But always they were in forest. The road they were
on finally was more sand than gravel—suddenly soft
and loose for a while, then crossed by hard corduroy
ridges. Sometimes the motorcycle seemed to be
swimming, sometimes to be bucking; it was hard to
concentrate.

They went straight past a few farmhouses, with
occasional barking dogs, and curved through pockets

of cool, damp air, around small swamps, and always went on into deep, dark "canyons" through more dense forest. Even after three years in that country, Arley wasn't used to how the woods crowded together and blotted out the sky. He couldn't see enough stars to keep track of which directions they were turning, and he couldn't get a good glimpse at his watch. He judged they hadn't been going quite an hour when they came to another railroad crossing. The girl drove over it and went on maybe two miles further, then she slowed and pulled to the side amid another long stretch of dark trees. She stopped, with the motor idling.

"Get off and wait for me here," she said quietly. "I've got to scout ahead. I'll be back soon."

Arley got off the cramped seat willingly.

"And listen to me—" she kept speaking to him, softly and quickly. "If I'm not back in twenty minutes, you sneak forward. About half a mile down there's an opening into an old logging trail, on the right. But you've really got to *sneak*. A half mile—on the right. Got that?"

Arley nodded and started to ask her—

But she stopped him. "*Listen:* that opening's hard to see at night. If you miss it, you'll come to some cleared pasture with a new-fixed gate. There'll be a truck parked, and maybe hid, just inside there."

"What kind of truck?" Arley hissed. "Whose?"

"A truck that can carry a horse. But it'll be unloaded by now. You'll have to find that trail—without anyone seeing you—and follow it: two miles straight into the woods. You'll come to a clearing with an old sawmill next to a lake. Your horse'll be hidden there, somewhere, with the guy who took him. You'll have to sneak around there to find him and get away."

"This is crazy," scowled Arley. "I want to know—"

"*Listen!*" she murmured, fiercely. "He's going to meet other men, so you've got to get there first. If I don't get back here, it's because he was still watching for me to follow him and caught me, so I'll probably be tied up somewhere. But he won't think I'd bring anyone else. And you can't lose much time looking for m—"

"Tied up by who?" Arley cut her short. "First you tell me—" he demanded, and grasped at her arm. But she throttled up as he spoke, clamped tightly to her handlebars, and churned away before he could get a good grip on her.

He ended stumbling along in the motorcycle's spray. Then, left alone, he began to think very quickly. First he squinted at his watch, which seemed to say it was a little past eleven. Then he looked at the ribbon of stars visible directly above the road, trying to get his bearings. It was almost like meeting a friend to recognize the bright bluish star near several small white ones that were spread out in a kind of long, bent cross. He knew that the cross was called "The Swan," and that he was seeing them glittering in the midst of the Milky Way. Together they told him the road he was on went east and west. That mean the railroad they'd crossed went north and south. So they were probably the same tracks they'd bounced along when they'd left the fairgrounds. But were they still north of Feast Lake, or had the turnings she'd made brought them around south of town?

The stars couldn't tell him that. In the near darkness he sniffed deeply, but his nose wasn't strong enough to tell him much. Free from the motorcycle's rumbling, he could hear constant rustlings in the treetops. A breeze was blowing that sent only light drafts down along the road—but were *all* those shifting noises just wind? His eyes became willing to see all kinds of things in the faint starlight shadows. It wasn't ghosts he thought of, it was a riled bear, or wolves, or people who got queer kicks out of luring kids off somewhere and then doing painful things to them.

Suddenly he didn't like where he was at all, or whatever it was he was up to. He wanted to kick himself for letting that girl rush him out here.

Without waiting twenty minutes, he started to

ease his way forward along the edge of the road, trying to peer ahead the half mile; he could see nothing except vague darkness. Whose target would he be if he tried to find that trail, or truck? If he tried to run off on the sandy road, he'd be in the open, leaving clear tracks. In the woods he'd likely soon get lost, and make a racket doing it. Maybe he was better off for now right where he was.

He reached hurriedly about at the brushy edge of the woods till he found a dead stick he might use as a club, then he worked himself a way into the brush and rested down on one knee. Now if something tried to sneak up on him, the brush would hide him, or at least rattle and warn him so he could fight.

What attacked immediately was mosquitoes, but he thought they might be better than some other things.

Abruptly from close behind and above him an owl's voice sang out—a hoarse, barklike sort of hooting—and like an echo from somewhere across the road another, partly muffled call answered. The near owl spoke loudly again and was answered once more. With shivers still tingling in his neck, Arley was trying to decide if the owls were as real as they sounded or were some kind of signal, when he heard the motorcycle coming back. He heard the machine pause, with the motor idling, right where she'd left him. After a few seconds more, he heard her call quietly, "All right. Let's go!"

Arley held still. Like the owls.

The girl's voice became agitated. "Can't you hear me?" she hissed louder. "Answer me. This isn't a game!"

What *is* it? Arley said to himself. And waited.

He heard the motorcycle go muttering slowly on. She's looking for tracks, he thought.

The muttering came slowly back and paused again right out there on the road. "There's no footprints," he heard her say. "You've *got* to be here. Answer me. Don't run out on me!" Her voice took on the same pleading urgency she'd used at the fair. "*Listen—* He'll *kill* your horse. When he's done, he'll take it to one of the swamps and use an axe. Silently. And let it sink out of sight. They've told him he's got to. So he will."

Arley's jaw clenched with anger, and his lips twitched with confusion over whether to believe and what to do.

"You've *got* to be hearing me," the girl exclaimed. "Answer me. *Hurry*. Or the moon'll come first. We've got to go!"

Arley wondered if moonlight would reveal him. For sure daylight would, and he'd still be on his own. In the meantime, what of Tug? He felt trapped. He couldn't stay hidden. "Go where?" He spoke out boldly, as abruptly and probably as hoarsely as the owl, and he heard the girl gasp at the sudden closeness of his voice.

"I'll show you!" she exclaimed. "C'mon. Don't snag us now. Let's get off the road before someone sees us."

What's wrong if someone does? Arley wondered, and stayed concealed. "First tell me who *he* is," he told her. "Who has my horse?"

"My— Someone I know," she answered quickly. "I overheard them talking. They didn't know I was there. Please, now, let's go!"

"*Who* was talking?" Arley wanted to know.

The motorcycle muttered then a little louder, its sound shifting about. He realized she was turning it around again. Now it would be facing back the way they'd come together. "*Listen*—" he heard her repeat, as the motor settled to idling. "He's got your horse by that sawmill. As soon as the moon's up—" At that moment the owl behind him cried out again, and then twice repeated its calling with the distant owl across the road, while the girl kept talking. "—a plane'll land on that lake, from Canada. They'll unload something, and he'll use your horse to pull it to the road. *Their* truck's going to be coming by here to get it. Then he's supposed to kill your horse so no one'll find it and wonder why it was stolen.

If the cops think it disappeared into some slaughter-house, they won't come nosing around here. Now will you believe me? Will you keep coming with me?"

The owls were silent, and Arley stayed hunkered quietly in the brush, but he felt more blinded by the darkness than concealed by it. Surely she knew just where he was. But he didn't know what to believe. He kept grasping the club, the mosquitoes were biting away, and his heart was pumping blood to them fast, urging him not to just stay there, a sitting duck, but to do something. Do something! But he wasn't going to go dashing off wildly and blindly again. He was going to know more than this. "What're they hauling?" he demanded.

The girl's voice snapped toward him with sharp impatience. "Listen, you, I've said plenty. And I don't know. They said Japanese cameras. Six hundred pounds of stolen new cameras. But it could be anything. They'd say anything. They're giving my—friend—six thousand dollars to help sneak it into this country. And we—he needs the money. Now that's enough talk! Please, the moon—in only an hour—"

But Arley decided to gamble even more time trying to learn still more, so he could make his own judgments. "Who are *you?*" he interrupted.

"No," she said. "You don't have to know that.

You just have to get your horse away. The moon rises in an hour, and we'll need every minute. I'm not joking. So stop delaying us!"

Suddenly Arley had an idea. If he got Tug back, her "friend" couldn't make six thousand dollars hauling anything. But a tough, strong girl with a motorcycle handy might make that money instead.

Was that possible? Was he getting yanked into a fight between crooks? How could he tell?

As he hesitated a second, trying to figure what might happen if he told her what he suspected, he heard a strange sound that could have been either a moan or a curse. Then she said, "I can't wait any more. If you won't come, I'll go try to get that horse away myself." Then again he heard the idle of the motor go stronger, and it began moving away.

Arley couldn't tell if she was faking or not. He decided rapidly that she might go without him, that he'd gain nothing staying blindly where he was, that for Tug's sake he couldn't take a chance on not going.

"All right, I'm coming." He spoke out quickly, pushed himself out from the brush, and made a run to get back on the motorcycle as it was starting away ahead of him. As he ran, something distracted him a moment—the busy rush of an owl flying swiftly across the road. Then he had to throw away his club in order to run faster and leap-frog over the rear wheel onto the seat, and get his grip around her waist. She had her helmet off.

"Where to?" he panted. "You said we've got to get to that lake."

"We'll sneak around by another trail," he heard her say. "I'll show you."

13

Leading a Horse to Water

THE TREETOPS KEPT SHIFT-
ing and chattering as the breeze kept passing through
them and dipping down across the sawmill meadow.
The breeze was rich with the tantalizing scent of
water. From behind one edge of the trees, waves
could be heard steadily lapping against a shore.
Everything seemed to be restless, everything teased
at Tug's thirst, while he kept patiently chewing at
all the meadow grass the snubbed halter rope would
let him reach.

He heard Yellow Cap start grunting from somewhere inside the dark, broken building where he had
disappeared. So Tug quickly rolled his tongue
around an extra bunch of grass, bit it off, and then

looked up. That way, by doing first things first, he could munch on a full mouthful as he looked and not lose any eating time to curiosity.

Also, Tug didn't raise his head very fast to look because his neck was still sore from the jolt it got when he'd had to plunge off the back of the truck. He saw Yellow Cap come out of the blackness into the starlight, all bent over, dragging something in much the same way a horse would. Behind him came something low and square-shaped.

Yellow Cap kept grunting as he towed the shape out into the open. It was the front part of an old-time logging sled. The two runners were of thick, stout oak nearly as long as a horse, rimmed with iron. The crossways bolster beam and blocks that braced the runners apart, and on which the front end of a load of logs would rest, were of even thicker wood.

With a similar set of runners hooked firmly behind to make a complete sled, a team of two horses, shod with cleated shoes, could pull over one hundred tons of logs in a single load—if they were on a winter road made of smoothed ice. But over that fallen rubble and dry lumpy ground, the runners dragged hard. Yellow Cap soon let go of it and came for Tug.

By now Tug was smelling the rusty metal and old cracked wood. He could tell what the equipment was, and as soon as Yellow Cap loosened the halter rope, Tug stood around into position to be hitched for hauling. He waited, as usual, for the light slap of the harness leathers to fall upon him, and he waited with all senses alert for another horse—because he knew that the long wooden tongue that stuck forward was meant to be hitched to a team.

Yellow Cap had no such things. Instead of a harness he simply undid coils of his rope and cut two lengths, which he tied in separate tight loops around Tug's neck. Then he lifted the pole-tongue along Tug's left side and tied it to the neck coils.

It wasn't a good arrangement, and Yellow Cap knew it. "This is all I've got, so it has to do," he growled, with a nervous excitement that was about the same thing as being angry. He snapped the loose end of the halter rope against Tug's hip and ordered: "All right, let's go. Pull it like it is. Or I'll spur you with an axe!"

Tug didn't understand the words. He sensed the threat in the man's tone, but everything about the man's scent and movements seemed mostly frightened. It didn't make any sense to Tug, and he didn't like the whip of the rope against him. So he stepped forward against the "harness" of ropes and began pulling. It was the only thing he knew to do.

The sled runners were not nearly as heavy for him to move as they had been for the man. Yet they

dragged enough over the dry ground for the strain
to hurt his sore neck, and for the splintery twists
of the rope strands to bite into his skin. It didn't
bother too much at first, but got a little worse with
each step. It was only pain, though. That didn't
alarm him like having to jump from the truck had
done. So Tug kept obeying. Sooner or later there
would be rest again, and water.

With Tug working, Yellow Cap became less
excited. "Good," he sighed. "Just keep going. Just
because I'm doing this, doesn't mean I like it. Understand?"

Tug didn't understand those words either. He
just heard the voice become softer.

Then for sure they were heading for water.
Using the halter rope, the man reined him closer to
the wave sounds and onto a narrow path downhill
through the trees. Faster than the man could direct
him, Tug maneuvered the long runners behind him
onto the path also. A breeze rushed at them as they
went down the path, and then there were no more
trees ahead or to the sides, and a full wind flowed
against their faces under a very wide starry sky.
Right in front of them was the lake. Its far shore
was a solid darkness jagged and low against the stars.
All the surface in between was filled with the rippling silvery edges of mild waves. Because of the
scant rain, the lake was low, and the incoming waves

could not reach the shore vegetation. Instead they foamed and chased each other with hissing and ploshing sounds along a bank of bare stones.

Yellow Cap kept walking right down those bare stones and into the lake, pulling on the halter rope for Tug to come too. The wet stones were slippery, and even more so for Tug on his nearly smooth metal shoes.

As soon as he could reach water, Tug paused and put his head down to drink. Again that kind of movement yanked Yellow Cap to a stop. Knee-deep in the lake, the man twisted around and this time whipped the loose end of the halter rope across Tug's nose. "Quit it! Keep moving! I gotta be ready before the moon's up!"

Tug, wide-eyed with surprise, jerked his head up and away from the rope lashing at his face—and felt another jolt of pain go through his sore neck. So he settled back to pulling, stepping deeper into the lake, holding his head just above the white flickering tops of the wet waves. Behind him the sled was now half afloat, while in front of him Yellow Cap stopped and with hurried swings of the halter rope and excited, barking orders got Tug to wade in a big circle around him.

Out that far the bottom was muddy, and with every swing of the rope, Yellow Cap's feet slipped and he had to struggle to stay upright against the push of the waves. All his movements were wild and unpredictable, while Tug, who could hold his great strength on three or four legs at once, and whose barrellike body got a lot of buoyant boost from the water, went steadily around him, towing the sluggishly floating sled. Then Tug calmly followed as Yellow Cap floundered back to shore.

Yellow Cap led him up over the bare stones and up the path until the trailing sled came just out of the water. Then he stopped and tied the halter rope to the nearest tree beside the path. Once again the man's excitement began to subside.

"Okay," he panted. "It's turned around. Ready to load and go." He turned his face directly at Tug's eyes. "Look, you," he said. "Just because I'm doing this doesn't mean I like it. I didn't make the problem, but *I've* got to solve it. Can you understand that? *You're gonna have to understand that!*"

Then Yellow Cap pushed quickly past between Tug and the trees. He went down to the shore and along it a short way, where he pulled a thin flat-bottomed boat from hiding and set it ready to be launched on the lake. From his knapsack he pulled two flares and set them each into the ground along the shore about fifteen feet apart, ready to be lighted as all-clear signals when the moon rose.

Tug couldn't see what the man was doing. Tied in the narrow pathway, where the crowded breeze was rushing past full of the teasing touch of moisture from the lake, he still had not gotten to drink. His thirst was beginning to feel like dry sand in his mouth. His neck was not only sore, but now its skin was burning where the coarse ropes of his "harness" had been constantly chafing. And the ropes still rubbed with every movement he tried to make.

But he expected that soon enough the work would end, and he would have water to drink and the burning would end. In the meantime Tug gingerly reached his head upward and began patiently munching on some tree leaves.

14

The Slough Chase

THE GIRL SPED THEM BACK along the road they'd come on—but just the two miles or so to the last railroad crossing. There she slowed suddenly and swung the motorcycle into a sharp left turn, steering straight between glimmering iron rails, the way she'd done when they sneaked away from the fair.

This time she kept her headlight on and throttled faster. Arley could see some of the bumps coming, though they were more severe. Again he had to grip the seat snugly with his knees, but had to loosen his grip around her waist so he could swing out his elbows to help keep his balance. Eventually a pale milepost appeared in the headlight glow and seemed to go jumping past. A little way later she slowed the motorcycle to another muttering pause.

"We turn again," she said, barely louder than the idling engine. "Let's get this bike off of here."

She had motioned with her left hand as she'd spoken. Arley could see nothing to *either* side, except the nearby dense darkness of the woods. "What's here?" he asked.

"Another trail, like I told you. It goes to that trail your horse went on. They meet at the mill clearing and lake. We're going to sneak in from this side."

Maybe there was a trail close by that he couldn't see in the dark. But there was still more he wanted to know. "What happens when we sneak?" he said sternly.

"I'll explain, when we have to get off again and walk."

"Why not *now?*"

"Because we've got to beat that moon. They're going to use moonlight to land by. *Please:* help me get this off of here so we can go!"

Her *please*, her sureness, the threat of an axe being swung at Tug . . . His questions, however rigidly he spoke, could not overcome those things. He felt compelled to grab the motorcycle and help it over a rail and down into tall, thin grasses, where they received a slow greeting from a few mosquitoes, who were sluggish in the night coolness. Automatically he got back on the seat, and immediately she throttled forward. The headlight seemed to start pushing a narrow tunnel right through the woods, which still seemed iron-black all around him. They couldn't be moving very fast, but the tall, thin grasses that filled the "tunnel" were reflecting brightly and making dizzying patterns, bending down this way and that as the motorcycle passed over them.

Arley fought to keep hold of his new sense of direction. They had made two left turns. By what the stars had told him, they'd first gone back east on the road, then north on the tracks, now west. They were traveling three sides of a square. The trail she said that Tug had taken would be the fourth side. They would come to a corner somewhere in these dark woods, at a sawmill clearing, by a lake. Then what?

On and on they seemed to go, as the frenzy, of those bending grasses stirred up Arley's excitement more and more.

Finally she stopped the motorcycle again, and this time switched off the motor. In the steady, motionless moment before she also flicked off the headlight, he saw a low, dark shape or shadow, which lay crossways ahead of them, and what seemed a gray bridge going over it. Then the light went out, and his eyes were left almost totally blind.

His other senses quickly became more alert. He again heard the rustling of a breeze through the treetops—it sounded like laughter there. And he scented a strong mixture of damp smells.

She stayed seated, because she was probably night-blind for a moment, too.

Again Arley had to ask, "What's here?"

"It's a slough that curves all through these woods. We'll have to get off and slog it."

"Why not keep on this trail?"

"Because it goes straight to that sawmill clearing, and Gregg could spot us coming. This bog angles right to the lake, and we can sneak along the shore."

Arley had caught the new word *Gregg.* "Who's Gregg?" he said abruptly; and nearly took her off guard.

"He's my— No." She halted. "You don't have to know that. I shouldn't have let his name slip. It doesn't matter. Oh, God!" she suddenly exclaimed, and lifting her legs she spun herself to the side and stood up away from the motorcycle. "I wish we were out here to build a fire and sing songs. But we're not. So come on," she ordered. "Let's keep going to get your horse."

But what had happened to his family on the plains gave Arley no reason to believe things always naturally worked out all right if you just kept going as you were. Her sharpness reminded him of that. Sternly again, he insisted, "Tell me how."

"As we go," she repeated. "Time's too short."

Arley's vision had improved enough that he was beginning to see stars in the open sky above the slough, but the woods around were still frustratingly blurry. He stayed astraddle the motorcycle, wondering how quickly he might start it up, and got irritated at not knowing whether he should. He wanted to get in charge of what was happening, but couldn't yet understand enough to make a decision. Angrily he demanded, "I want to know first."

Again she threatened to go without him. "Listen, you!" she snapped. "Right now there's just one guy to beat. If that moon gets up there'll be more. I'm starting now whether you—"

For Arley that threat had come once too often. This time he boiled up at being pulled around in the dark. He didn't delay to say any more, but she must have recognized his intentions for she turned and ran and got a few steps headstart as he came storming off the motorcycle. He meant to grab her some way and force his answers from her, but she went leaping down off the trail beside the gray bridge and disappeared beneath it.

ARLEY HELD BACK and ducked to one side, aware that she might be trying to lead him into an ambush.

From where he crouched amid the grasses, he could make out the bridge in the slough's starlight fairly clearly. It stretched across the dip of the slough's channel, spanning the channel's entire width without a single post to help it. Its beams seemed to be made of tree trunks, longer and thicker than any Arley had ever seen. Then he heard soft squnching sounds that made him guess the girl was moving away along the slough from the other side of the bridge.

He wanted to let her go, he wanted to head back for the railroad on the motorcycle, if the key was there, or on foot if he had to; again he wanted to get away from whatever he'd gotten mixed up in. But he saw in front of him a ghostly vision of old Tug looking back at him, friendly and dependable, ready to take another load of logs through the stump fields. He saw the flash of a ghostly axe, swinging at the horse's head in the darkness. As before, he couldn't desert Tug. Instead he burst out in pursuit of the girl.

Arley could hear only the soft thunking of his own feet and the hissing of his breathing as he ran; but ahead in the lumpy, treeless channel, he could see a flickering that more or less kept a constant shape. As he gained a little on it, he was sure it was her. She was springing from hummock to hummock and missing the mucky spots more smoothly than he was. Though he was trim, light, and strong, he was working harder for his own speed and gaining only a little by it. He began to wonder if he could keep going when the girl disappeared once more, around a curve.

When he reached the same bend he saw that the slough was heading for a dead end. No—not a dead end. It was a dead tree fallen across the channel. A tree not nearly as big as the ones in the bridge, but with a great mass of branches barring passage. The girl was trying to claw and slip her way through them, and he swung his arms harder and drove his legs to go faster.

He could hear her still scraping and crackling branches as he reached the tree; and the opening she'd made let him force through a little easier, gritting against small, sharply broken limbs that scraped his shins and poked his ribs. For a few moments he felt the panic a bear might feel, trapped in a wooden cage, then he broke his way out on the other side, only a few steps behind her, and he knew he would catch her.

She swung around to meet him and faked one way then tried to dodge the other. She was tired, and the ground was soft; it didn't work. He caught her blouse and his hand touched something very hard beneath the cloth as he pivoted and aimed his shoulder against her and they fell together. She was older and strong, but he was much more experienced at play-yard brawling and was quickly kneeling astride her, forcing her hands down, trying to get enough breath to demand all the information he'd need. She was struggling for wind too, her stomach tightening and flattening beneath him. He remembered the hard shape in her blouse. The blouse had been pulled loose and he saw the handle of a knife, which he yanked from under the waistband of her jeans. "What's this for?" he gasped.

"Listen." With his weight on her, her voice was practically gagging. "We can't—fight ourselves—we've got to—beat him!"

"With *this?*"

"It's to—cut your horse free—he'll have him—hitched by ropes—to a drag."

"Who's *him?*" His anger was riling up again. He wanted to squeeze the hands he held and bounce on her to force out answers. But he was still too winded, so he just sat tightly and growled, "*Tell me!*"

But she didn't. "He'll have—a boat there," she panted. "A duck boat—you know those?"

He recognized that that was information he could use. "Like a canoe. Only flat-bottomed," he muttered.

"He'll use it—to haul—stuff from the plane—to the drag—for your horse to pull—to the road."

"Six hundred pounds, and some guy—all in a duck boat?"

"He'll make two trips—or tow it swimming—I tell you he's strong."

"While he's swimming, I get to get Tug?"

"*Before.* Before there's any other—men there—to help him!"

"How do I know he's alone?"

"*I* know. And he won't think—that I'll bring anyone. So I'll go ahead." Her voice was gradually getting steadier. "I'll try to tow off the boat, or start an argument. While he's fussing at me, you get your horse! It's got to be that quick and simple, or it won't work. Now get up! We've got to get there before that moon—"

To Arley it still didn't make whole sense. "How do you escape?" he interrupted.

"I can swim if I have to."

"Suppose he grabs you?"

"It won't matter. He won't really hurt me. He's my—" She stopped, and exclaimed, "Let me up! We've got to go!"

She didn't seem old enough to be married. "He's your *brother*," Arley challenged.

"All right! So you know. That's why I can't call the cops. I don't want him in jail. If we get your horse away, he'll *have* to quit it and run. He won't be able to haul the stuff and get arrested."

"He could still use the boat."

"No. There's no road anywhere near to this lake. And the slough's too low. So he stole your horse. I was afraid to try to stop him too soon. I was afraid he'd go to some plan I didn't know anything about." Then she squirmed hard to get free and snarled sharply, "Let's get up and go!"

But Arley still saw dark corners to her story, so he would not let loose of his leverage. "How come I don't remember you from school?"

She kept squirming. "We go another way."

Arley locked his knees tighter around her waist and pushed harder on her hands. He felt he had to learn who she was, that he had to know it *all*, before he tried to beat smugglers in strange country in the dark. "Up at Rune?" he persisted.

"It doesn't matter where!" she hissed, fiercely. "We're losing time!"

Arley stared down more closely at her smooth face. The fine round curve of her chin was now wider, because her jaw was clenched and her lips drawn back from her teeth with strain. Yet there was something familiar about her face that he couldn't pin down. Another mystery still scraping at him as she stopped squirming, but in the same instant she started vigorously trying to roll and shake herself free. It took all his strength to hold her, but she didn't have the strength or know-how to get him off.

"Where's your parents?" Arley kept after her.

"Listen, *please!*" she exclaimed, and stopped struggling to put all her effort into her voice: "My father's had a stroke. He needs treatment to keep him from shriveling up. But that costs, and it's got to be done soon, and this has been a lousy year for crops. Everything's piled on us, so we've got to sell out. Only Gregg won't give up, not since this friend of his, who's become a pilot, came back with this secret idea for smuggling stuff. Now Gregg's setting himself up to go to prison, and if my father finds out, the shock will kill him. And I'm just trying to keep it from happening!"

There was something else familiar—terribly familiar—to Arley as she spoke up at him about sickness and selling out. She kept sounding more and more believable. Even so one piece kept refusing to fit: "But why *axe the horse?*" he exclaimed.

"I don't know!" It was almost a yell. She was just barely keeping her voice under control: "They've just told him to. They said if he didn't get rid of all evidence, either the cops would be after him or they would. He's scared enough to do it. Even if they don't show up or land, he's supposed to do it. So, *please*, let me up. Let's go! We haven't—

You fat-headed clod! See what you've done! Let me up! Let me up! See what's happened! See my face! *Let me up!*"

Suddenly she'd begun struggling at him again, and her voice was rapidly biting up at him in a frantic anger. Arley automatically fought her down in self-defense, but he saw her face as he did so. It seemed to glow for him. He saw that his hand holding hers seemed to glow. And the slough grasses they were sprawled in were much paler, but only in splotches. He saw that dark shadows were spilling down on the channel around them from an edge of the trees, and everywhere between the shadows the air had a weak milky clearness. He realized that low beyond the trees the night's bright half-moon had risen.

OF COURSE the moon would've risen anyway. It proved nothing. Arley had no more proof of what she was saying than he'd ever had. In fact, he had no proof that the spectral light in the woods was from the moon. But he didn't doubt that it was. And right then each thing she'd told him seemed suddenly to fit squarely with everything else she'd told him. She seemed as genuine as that owl's voice had been by the road. Arley let loose of her and stood immediately, taking up the knife as he did and jamming it handle-first into a hip pocket, and complaining, "Why didn't you tell me all this right off?"

She was quickly up beside him. "I *said* I'd tell as we went," she complained, as they began again running awkwardly along the slough. Only this time they were together.

"Even a horse won't lead everywhere blind," Arley muttered.

"You spook so easy, you probably wouldn't have come at all," she snapped back.

"Let's not fight now," he said.

"That's what I told you before."

You should've told me everything before. We'd be further along, Arley kept thinking, but didn't say it. His wind was quickly short again, and the moonlight that let him see easier where to put his feet, also goaded him with the fear that they were already going to be too late. The continuing effort of leaping mud holes and striding through hummock grasses that were bent over and intertwined as toughly as fish netting soon made it impossible to think much, or even to be scared. Ahead he saw another tree fallen across the slough. They attacked it together. He wrestled aside a stout rubbery branch so she could get by, then escaped the back-snap of the branch as she made a way for him to scoot forward. Cooperation was a luxury. Yet it felt familiar, like something he hadn't known for a long time—not since that afternoon with Tug among the tar buckets.

When they got through the tree, they could hear, despite the breeze-rustled branches overhead, the splashing of waves along a shoreline. Yet they couldn't help but pause to rest and breathe.

She murmured, and her voice was mellower than before: "I'm sorry—this is happening—believe me."

"I believe it," he panted.

"Just because—Gregg listened—to that rotten pilot—everything's gone rotten."

"We're apples in a barrel." He nodded.

"We're *not* apples," she objected. "Maybe we can get out of the barrel."

"That's what we're trying. So let's go."

"Yes. C'mon."

In that way they urged their legs forward and leaned more than sprang into more weary running. Soon they pushed single-file through some mosquito-thick bushes to stand on an apron of dry marl, with the mosquitoes suddenly gone and the breeze full in their faces. Low bubbly-topped waves were coming busily against the shore a little out in front of them. The entire open spread of the lake was alive with small faintly flashing whitecaps and constantly flowing movements, while the entire sky with its bright half-moon gleaming just above the treetops seemed, by comparison, oddly motionless.

"Stay hidden," she hissed at him. "Let me go look alone. If there's two signal flares showing, there's no plane landed yet."

Arley waited impatiently. And the girl looked different to him, now that he believed they were working together. Standing out in the moonlight, with the breeze rippling her pale hair, she looked even prettier than before.

She came hurrying back. "I see the flares."

"Okay," he said. "Let's get Tug."

"Wait!" she grabbed his arm. "There's more you've got to know."

"Like what?"

"There's young trees grown up all along the shore. But there's a thin path up to the sawmill. That's where your horse is. Take him up to the clearing, then past a building with a broken chimney. That'll take you to the old road, the one we left the bike on. There's other old trails in the woods, but the one we used is the only one that goes to the railroad tracks."

"Okay, I'll—"

"Wait!—when you get back to that slough, where the bike is, don't cross that bridge. Go across through the bog. When you get to the railroad tracks turn right. I bet you can get back to the fair before daylight. You won't have to tell anyone you've been gone."

"You said there were trains after midnight," Arley remembered.

"You'll have to watch out and get aside. It's better'n leaving him to get axed. Now let's go."

"Yes," Arley agreed, and left the bushes in another run, close behind her. They went along the shoreline, and maybe a quarter mile away he could see two tiny red flares burning. Their feet left the slough's marl and began striking sand. To keep hidden as much as possible, they had to move as close as possible along the edge of the woods where the low water hadn't reached for a long time and the sand was dry and soft. Arley's strained ankles began to ache and his calf muscles were threatening to knot. He wondered if the girl was suffering in the same way. As they got closer to the flares, she'd have to go faster ahead alone, to confront her brother, then he'd have to sprint forward to find a thin trail and Tug and get him loose. At least the sounds of the waves coming in and the breeze stirring the trees were hiding the scrape of their footsteps.

But abruptly clear amid those sounds, he heard a steady humming that got rapidly closer, and in the next moment the dark bulk of a plane rushed from over the treetops, right above their heads. The humming at that moment became a loud buzz that turned into a dimming whistle as the plane sank even lower and went out where they could see the moonlight reflecting on it. There it kicked up two white glistening fans of spray when its pontoons found the waves.

Fortunately it'd had to come down into the wind, away from shore. But Arley guessed it could need less than three minutes to turn around and taxi to those flares. So now that was all the time they had.

FOUR

Moonlight
Emergencies

15

Nap Time

THE MAN DOWN BY THE shore had been fidgeting as busily as the waves, but Tug no longer gave him much notice.

The jerkily tied halter rope had come loose from the tree he'd been tied to, and he'd tried to get back to those waves to drink. But the long pole-tongue from the sled runners wouldn't bend out of his way, and it wasn't in his nature to purposely break things. So Tug no longer gave much attention to the water, either.

A few mosquitoes were sheltering by his chest, out of the wind, and they were biting at the raw places made by the chafing neck ropes. Those mosquitoes he ignored by keeping busy eating. With the halter rope loose, he could slowly move his sore neck in most directions; and with the long reach of his neck, he was quietly and calmly harvesting a great many tasty leaves.

Those trees, close beside the narrow path, were preventing him from seeing the moon, which had made no noise or smell as it rose. He couldn't see the flares either, though he could hear them fizzing and smell the bitter smoke of their chemicals. He didn't let it bother him. He'd been near marker flares once or twice before in his eighteen years.

A buzzing noise that had suddenly cut across the wind made him perk his ears a moment. That sound had quickly gone further away, and now the wind off the lake was carrying a thrumming kind of noise from out on the water. Tug had heard airplanes before, and all kinds of motors. These didn't seem to have anything to do with him.

He reached up a little higher for the next tasty group of leaves, and he heard a high-pitched human voice cry out: "Gregg! Get out of here!"

With his head raised, Tug could see behind him as well as if his head were turned. He saw Yellow Cap jump past the opening of the path, the way he'd seen rabbits jump up from the edge of bushes.

The man jumped like a rabbit, but gave a sharp growling bark like a dog: "What're you doing here? They're on the lake. They're coming!"

"Get away, Gregg! Stop being crazy!"

"Get out of sight! I told them no one else knew!"

Tug couldn't understand the words, but knew the voices were excited and angry. They also didn't seem to concern him. He peacefully bit off the leaves he was reaching for, though his ears flickered with continuing curiosity. From out on the lake he heard the airplane motor rev down and begin moving toward shore with the waves.

"This'll kill Dad. So quit it!" he heard the high voice yell.

"We *can't* quit!" the man barked. "*Hey*—get away from that boat!"

Then Tug saw the girl. She was waist-deep in the moonlit water, a boat starting to follow behind her. He saw Yellow Cap go charging into the water. The girl dove out of sight. Abruptly, from closer-by, Tug caught the sound and scent of someone else. The scent was familiar: it was the boy he'd been working with for several seasons.

The boy came running from along the shoreside trees into the pathway. He smelled of fear as strongly as Yellow Cap had, and that made Tug uneasy again. Tug kept his big head high, eyes wide. He stood with his huge long muscles tensed.

Waist-deep in the lake, Yellow Cap was grabbing hold of the boat, then he stumbled and wrenched around. There was a bubbly cry as he fought with something beside him. The boat swung loose, and the waves pushed it back against the shore.

Meanwhile the boy had come up next to Tug, and something was glinting like ice in the boy's hand, then the rope holding the pole-tongue tight along Tug's side popped loose. The tongue dropped away. The boy shoved the knife into his pocket and grabbed the halter rope. He tried to yank Tug forward by the rope, and hissed, *"Let's go!"*

But Tug stiffened his neck and held it braced against the threat of more jolts. He didn't want to follow where fear wanted to lead him.

Another movement caught Tug's eye as the airplane came into his vision, still a little way off-shore but still coming closer. It was bobbing slightly among the waves like a big and patient, or cautious, duck.

At the same time the boy's voice was a swift, desperate whisper—*"C'mon"*—as he ran at Tug, leaped up, and Tug felt the boy's grip and weight pull at his mane. Then the boy dug his boot toes into the neck ropes and swung himself further up and onto Tug's high back.

"Hey! You! Stop!" Yellow Cap's voice roared behind them. Now he was turning to charge toward shore, still almost hip-deep on the slippery stones. The girl was trying to leap along beside him. She seemed to shove him. He fell, and she tumbled down too.

Because of all the commotion, Tug still held his head high, but with the boy on his back the pull of the halter rope on his neck had ended, and as the boy's heels began scraping and knocking against his ribs, Tug began to amble forward, up the path, the way he'd done on the streets in the parade.

The boy kept kicking at his ribs and making anxious sounds, so old Tug began to amble faster. Behind him Yellow Cap and the girl sank into the water like two frogs, and Tug saw the glittering blur of the propeller in front of the airplane as it bobbed in larger and closer toward shore. It was all Tug saw of that, for he lowered his head in order to duck some low branches, and with the boy shifting about, trying to cling to his bare back, he went at a slow trot up the rest of the path and out onto the grassy clearing. The moonlight was gleaming there, showing parts of the old buildings more plainly and putting dark shadows around other parts.

Tug felt a slight pull from the halter rope, which the boy still held. It steered him toward one of the old buildings, and there in deep shadow, beside a pile of stones fallen from a thick chimney, Tug obediently, and willingly, halted.

"Do you think anyone in that plane saw us?" the boy murmured. "I heard a yell at first, like somebody drowning. Was it the girl or her brother? Should we just leave her?"

Tug could give no answers, though for a few moments he stood alertly, ears twitching, nostrils wide, eyes high, because the boy seemed so excited. He could smell nothing unusual. The breeze kept brushing by as before. The light splashing sounds from the waves along the shore they'd just left were almost as steady as the light whirring sound he could still hear from the airplane's motor. Tug could detect nothing to be excited about. He would've very much liked a drink, but he wasn't inclined to fuss for it. He started to lower his head to munch at some of the grasses that had sprung up around the fallen chimney stones, but the boy yanked at him to keep his head up.

"Stay alert, will ya," the boy whispered urgently.

To save his neck from more jolts Tug didn't try to graze again. While the boy sat tensely on him, trying to figure what he should do next, Tug set his legs as comfortably as he could and closed his eyes to catch a snooze.

16

Challenge in the Shadow

ARLEY SAT ON TUG, hearing the steady whining from the propeller amid the sounds of the breeze. He told himself moment by moment that he and Tug ought to be finding that trail back to the railroad and getting as far away as they could, fast.

But that wild bubbling yell he'd heard, when he'd been hurrying to cut Tug loose, still rang in his mind. He'd been too busy at the time to hear it well. Had she screamed, or her brother?

Either way, she might need help. She'd been helping him get Tug back. Now he ought to see if she was safe.

On the other hand, people yelled from excitement, as well as pain or danger. Suppose she'd gotten away—then to go back would ruin everything.

So he ought to go on—

Except, now he heard, briefly, the breeze-carried ripple of men's voices.

Suppose she hadn't gotten away? What would her brother and those men be doing to her for interfering with them? Yet it'd be stupid to just rush back like some comic book hero and try to overpower them. His thoughts rattled and swung like the treetops around the clearing.

He'd better wait, he decided. When the plane was gone, he'd sneak back to see if she needed help.

But suppose some men were still there, to haul their stuff by hand? No, six hundred pounds would be too heavy for men to carry far. Unless they made several trips, which would take a long time. They'll fly it away again, or hide it till— Maybe he could find it, and hide it from them so the cops—

He heard the engine rev up, then it made a droning roar. That droning sounded odd because it seemed to be going away, yet it was getting louder. Of course: the plane was working to take off, into the waves and wind. The droning became softer. It was airborne.

He had to wait a bit more in the shadow, Arley decided. To be sure the plane didn't swing back over the clearing and maybe see him moving in the moon-light. Later, he'd hide Tug in those trees and sneak on through the trees to shore.

As he waited, he noticed that the droning sound wasn't fading. Instead it seemed to be circling around. What did that mean?

Tug's head suddenly raised, with his ears rigid, aiming toward the narrow path from the shore. Arley heard Tug make a questioning sniff. Icily he wondered who else might've heard that. He had gripped the halter rope and lifted his heels, ready to snap and kick Tug into a run, when he saw some-thing flickering out in the clearing. At first it looked like just a startled deer breaking cover, but it didn't move fast enough. He realized it was the girl, run-ning toward him.

She was going to run past him.

"*Hey,*" he hissed.

"*Oh!*" she gasped, as she sprang sideways. "You!" she exclaimed louder and came running at him so quickly Arley had only a second to wonder what she intended doing. She stopped beside Tug's raised head. "What—are you *doing here?*"

She looked thin as a deer, with her pale hair and darker clothing all wet and plastered close against her.

Arley said, "I heard a yell like maybe you—"

"Oh, thank god! I thought I was going to have to try to get the bike across the bridge. Come, quick —we've got to get him."

"Who?"

"Gregg. He's hurt. We've got to get him out of here!"

"What happened? What's going on?"

"I'll tell you. Come with me. Please. Hurry!"

Arley realized he'd gotten roped in like that before. Yet again she seemed urgently in need of him, and her face was just as pretty with her hair clinging round it in the moonlight. He held the halter rope he was using as reins and stayed put, but he asked, "Who yelled like they were drow—"

"I couldn't help it. I tried to fight for the boat, but he shoved me under and grabbed it. When he turned back around, he must've seen you."

"I heard him shout to stop."

"All I could do was run after him and shove. I got him to trip. He wrenched his knee. That bottom's all rock. We had to crawl away and keep hiding under water. He got scared about what they'd do if they found he wasn't ready for them. Now his knee's so swollen he can't even get all the way out. So we've got to get him. Let's go."

"Just wait," said Arley. "Who else is there?"

"No one. Just Gregg, and he's too hurt and scared now to hurt you. Believe me!"

"That plane—" Arley began.

"Didn't you hear it take off? They're all gone." She was talking rapidly but very clearly, in a military way that went odd with the softness of her wide cheeks and the fine smooth dip of her chin. "But we heard who they were. One guy got out and called. He didn't use Gregg's name, and it wasn't Gregg's friend. We wouldn't have answered anyway. Then another guy got out. They were cops. They must've captured the others in Canada and were hoping to trap the rest of the gang here. But when no one answered, they got scared to come ashore. I heard them radio that they might get shot in the dark. They told some other guys in cars to call for more police to block all the roads. They were going back up to scout from the air. Listen! you can still hear the plane. But if they can't find Gregg here, maybe they can't pin anything on him. We can get Gregg on that sled, and your horse can pull him to the bike. Then we can all get back to town. We can say we never left, that he hurt his knee there."

"We can't go that fast along tracks," Arley objected. "It'll get daylight too quick."

"It's not as far back as you think. I made some extra turns coming out here so you couldn't remember where we were."

"But that plane—"

"We won't use any lights, and there'll be shadows across the tracks. Anyway it's a *chance!*"

"Yeah, a chance they'll find Tug and me trying to sneak out. That'll make 'em think we were part of this from the start."

"We'll tell them not."

"They'll believe what they see. Why should they believe you? They'll know a horse was there. They'll find his droppings. And hairs. He's probably lost hairs on the brush. Even if we get to town, they'll match hairs."

"With what horse? The ground's too grassy or hard for good tracks. Where'll they look? At a kid's horse at the fair? Why should they?"

"And why should I help him?" Arley finally said bluntly. "He stole my horse and would've killed him and really was trying to smuggle."

"You've got your horse back!" Suddenly she was no longer very military, but snarling and glaring like a large cat ready to spring up at him. "I could've just hid and shot this horse back there where he got unloaded. Gregg would've had to quit his scheme right there. He wouldn't even be here, and the bears would be eating fresh horsemeat. But I've gambled to save your horse, too, and now maybe Gregg's scared enough that he's *through* doing stuff like this; but now you've got your horse so you want to run out on me."

Seated on Tug, Arley was quite a bit above her,

but not far enough, and he had nowhere to turn to escape the barbs of truth that again seemed to be in what she said. He was silent as he tried to reason out if the truth was actually like she said.

She kept after him, but with a voice starting to mellow again: "Don't you have any brothers or sisters?" she asked. "Hasn't anyone in your family had any trouble? Or needed your help?"

Arley didn't bother to answer that. It was no longer the moonlight on her pretty face that was bothering him. He could still hear her frightened yell from the lake, and he could still see clearly a vision of Tug being chopped open, or shot, if she hadn't brought him here. This was different than being asked to go out in twenty below zero to haul logs so his parents could pay some bills. She wasn't offering any job he could feel good about when he reached his warm supper. She was after him for a favor owed, and Arley felt that to ever be free of her, he must accept the challenge.

"All right," he said. "Let's go get him."

17

The Moonlight Retreat

Tug ENJOYED A SENSE OF relief when the girl, standing right below his ears, and the boy, sitting on him right behind his ears, quit arguing. He made no objection to being urged forward then and willingly let himself be guided across the clearing toward the narrow path, toward water—

There was the lake, again just several steps ahead of him. But once more no one seemed to think he was thirsty. The boy stopped him short and hurriedly made him turn around at the edge of the shore stones. Then the boy slid off and began lashing the sled's pole-tongue once more to the ropes still around Tug's neck.

Yellow Cap came hobbling out of the water, leaning heavily on the girl. Tug had seen injured men at the lumber camps where he'd worked, so there was nothing new about that. No one was saying much, but everything they did say, and all their movements, everything about them, seemed still tense and fearful. Tug couldn't completely ignore that; he stayed alert, but confused, for he could neither hear, see nor smell anything to be worried about.

The only thing that bothered him was thirst—and then, also, the returning bite of ropes into his shoulders as the boy ordered him to start hauling the sled up the path.

Then: "*Hold it,*" the boy commanded quietly, and Tug immediately stopped.

"These ropes'll cut him up," Arley hissed to the others.

"I know. But we don't have any padding," said the girl. "It'll take too long to strip bark."

From where he lay on the sled, drenched and starting to shiver with chill and pain, her brother argued, "It won't be a mile to that slough. He's got to keep going."

"The ropes'll hurt," Arley snapped. And then he admitted he had another worry beside Tug's welfare: "They'll leave marks. Someone might notice and wonder. Well, I've got a shirt." He began jerking it and his T-shirt up over his head. "Get his off too," he ordered the girl.

"We've got to keep hurrying," her brother kept urging.

"Well, get your arms out straighter so the sleeves'll come," she told him. Then as Arley finished winding his own shirts underneath part of the ropes around Tug's neck, she tossed him her brother's, and began undoing her blouse.

Arley couldn't help it. He had no sisters. In spite of himself, and the worry about being caught, the thought of the girl undressing there made him shift uncomfortably, and automatically he started to gesture that she didn't have to—

"If you don't want to see, keep your eyes closed," the girl told him. "I've got a bra on. It's no different from a bathing top."

Feeling challenged by her yet again, Arley purposely stood staring as her smooth strong shoulders came bare, and he remembered how he'd felt rude when she'd seen him just glancing at her while she was spying on Tug in the fair barn. Then the soggy blouse came flying at his face, and he almost missed it, but grabbed it and tucked it, too, beneath the neck ropes. Angry as much at his own clumsy embarrassment as at everything else, Arley next grabbed the halter rope and began leading up the path.

TUG SAW THEIR PALE SKIN and the girl's white bra glow in the moonlight, felt the helpful padding of their clothing beneath the ropes. Then, at a tug on the rope, he put his attention to skillfully dragging the sled with Yellow Cap on it up the path. Even though it was uphill and away from water, with ropes biting into him, Tug worked without complaint. Hauling was normal, this was action he understood. He powered his big feet across the slick grass, then the lumpy ground of the clearing, past the old building with the tall broken chimney, and onto a different trail through the woods than the one he'd come by. On the trail, branches reached over him; the moonlight became much dimmer, and the breeze was again only a busy rustling overhead. Mosquitoes slowly began to gang about him. The boy and girl began swinging their pale arms about, and Tug understood perfectly what they were doing. He heard groans from where Yellow Cap clung to the jouncing bolster beam across the runners.

Above the treetop rustlings he heard again the droning of the airplane. Tug peaceably ignored it. It meant nothing to him. He ignored the painful chafing of the ropes, whose hard twists were pressing through the cloths. Obediently he kept pulling along the trail, because at the end of every job, whenever it did end, there'd always been relief, and more feed and *water*.

Soon a damp, earthy scent told him there was more slough ahead. Mixed in that scent was a thin aroma of metal and oil: machinery. Tug was used to those kinds of smells.

When he got to the slough, he saw there was only one channel to go across, and it had a bridge.

"Go around. Don't go on the bridge," the girl hissed.

"Why not?" Arley kept his voice low, but he wanted an answer to that too. "Those beams are a yard thick," he pointed.

"You see any *standing* trees that thick?" she whispered. "They were all cut down eighty years ago."

As the talk ended, the boy led him to the side, to go around the bridge, and Tug followed eagerly, hoping to find a puddle to drink. But there was only mud, and heavy, squishing, painful, soggy labor to drag the sled through that mud. In the effort, the coarse ropes wore strips of the padding completely away. But the moment they were across the slough, the boy cut him loose from the tongue again. All the ropes were cut loose. The leftover smarting around his neck and shoulders seemed like nothing, compared to the pain when he'd been pulling.

So while the boy and girl pushed and shoved to get the motorcycle machinery turned around on the trail, Tug immediately rubbed against the closest brush to scour off the mosquitoes, and maybe the smarting too if he could, but he couldn't. Then matter-of-factly he stretched his hind legs and, de-spite his thirst, urinated over a gallon, scenting the air with ammonia. After which he took the oppor-tunity to munch at the grass and leaves about him as he nosed about looking for water, though finding only mud.

ARLEY STEPPED into the bushes to relieve himself as well. The need hit everyone, and when they all hur-riedly regrouped, wearing shirts now ragged and slick with horse sweat, they noticed that the buzz of the airplane had faded away. The breeze moving through the treetops was sounding very rhythmic and natural, the pause had broken their whole mood, so that it was getting hard for Arley, who'd been up since dawn, almost twenty-four hours, to stay alert and to keep believing there was danger really threatening. The girl was helping her brother onto the motorcycle, and Arley took the moment to breathe deeply and get himself ready to jump at

Tug's mane and clamber again onto the tall back, this time using Tug's bony joints, instead of neck ropes, for toeholds.

In that moment the moonlight beaming down through the open sky above the slough touched the brother's face, and the details he saw reminded Arley forcefully of the collision he'd had at the door to dim fair barn. He saw the brother's wide cheeks, the curved dip of his jaw, and the pale hair, so much like his sister's there close beside him. Now he knew why, when he'd seen her so soon after the collision, he'd thought the girl looked like someone familiar. There went that mystery.

Then the girl quickly slid onto the cycle seat, and Arley flinched as she started the motor. It reminded him of what they were up against, and he felt certain that anyone within ten miles must hear it.

Arley shook himself into action and scaled onto Tug's back. He tried to tell himself the cycle's slow mutter wasn't all *that* loud, and the wind sounds would absorb it. They started toward the railroad as fast as the motorcycle could manage with its load and no headlight on the old trail. Just about two miles to go, and they'd be on the tracks. Just twelve miles more, the girl promised, and they'd reach the fairgrounds; they could be there before daylight. Then he'd just have to somehow sneak a heavy horse quietly into the barn, make Tug look smooth before anyone looked at him, and then somehow keep himself from looking suspicious when he slept all morning.

They went only a short ways—less than a quarter mile—before Tug raised his head, ears cocked forward. Arley saw the signal and immediately hissed loudly, "Hold up! Something's ahead!"

As the motorcycle halted, a glow began to appear from the distance down the grassy trail. They thought that possibly it was just a strong shaft of moonlight from a break in the treetops, until it began growing noticeably stronger, as if some ghostly wagon lit with lanterns was coming jerkily over its route of long ago.

That illusion quickly dissolved.

"It's headlights!"

"Someone's coming!"

"Get out of sight!"

18

Hiding and Riding

THE APPROACH OF VE-
hicle lights was not unusual or alarming to Tug.

But being told to suddenly plunge off a trail
into thick, dark woods and brush was unusual, and
he knew it would be uncomfortable, so he hesitated.
However, when the boy's kicking and urgent voice
insisted, Tug closed his eyes against the poking tips
of branches and forced his heavy, solid chest against
the brush, which bent and gave way and let him
through, as the boy slid off beside him.

The boy stopped him and held Tug's head away
from the trail so the edge of the headlights' glare
would not reflect in his eyes. Nearby, the girl lay

sprawled over the motorcycle she'd ridden down off the side of the trail and rammed into the brush. She was trying to keep the silver handlebars from reflecting. With several sharp, moist, involuntary grunts of pain, Yellow Cap had purposely tumbled off the cycle and now was curled up as deeply in the brambly shadows as he could get.

On the trail a four-wheel-drive Ford Bronco bumped and squeaked closer, and closer, and went past. In the general glow of its headlights, the outline of siren lights atop it and a vague blotch like a police emblem on its door could be seen. Tug didn't understand any of this. He just stood perplexed and uncomfortable and patient but eager to turn around and be led back to some calmer, more open place, with *water.*

Then the three people near him began talking in quiet but quickly snapping voices that sounded like a pile of dry wood starting to burn.

"Hey, good," Yellow Cap's voice crackled first. "Now they're behind us. We won't meet them. Get that bike back on the trail."

"I need help pushing," the girl's voice hissed.

"Start it and *drive* it up there," Yellow Cap snapped.

"No," said the boy. He dropped the halter rope and started breaking through brush toward the girl.

"They'll hear it."

"They won't hear it till they get out at the bridge," said Yellow Cap. "Hurry up!"

The motorcycle suddenly started and muttered briskly, without moving.

"It *will* roar too loud driving up there. We've still got to push," said the girl.

Tug heard a mixture of gruntings and scrapings as the mild motor rumblings moved up out of the woods. Then the boy returned and took the halter rope and Tug followed with big strides as the boy led him out and back up onto the trail. There the motorcycle was making more constant mutterings, and Yellow Cap, again leaning heavily on the girl, was hopping up toward it.

"We've still *got* to be quiet," the girl was saying. "They'll get out at the bridge to sneak to the lake afoot, and they'll hear us."

"They *won't* hear us, with all the tree noises," Yellow Cap grunted.

"Or they might be coming back any moment," the boy said quickly.

"It'll take 'em a bit to turn around there." Yellow Cap spoke through clenched teeth as he reached for the cycle seat, and hopped onto it. "We can keep ahead of them. Let's go!" his voice crackled.

"I wonder if they know about that bridge," the girl murmured. She got on the seat too, in front of Yellow Cap.

"They know about this road, don't they. Let's go!" Yellow Cap crackled again. "Whatever they do, let's get long gon—"

He was cut off by a ripping sound, then a duller hammerlike *shunk,* none of it loud, but sudden and distinct. Tug raised his head and aimed his ears toward the noises. The first one had sounded like a tree falling. He didn't understand the second, and listened for more of it.

"*The bridge,*" the girl gasped.

"They've gone *through.*" The boy's voice sizzled like escaping steam.

Tug could hear no more of the noises, yet because of the tenseness of the people he kept listening.

"Well—it's—a soft bottom." Yellow Cap's voice was now not so crackling.

But the girl snapped: "It wouldn't fall straight down. It'd tip and roll."

The boy added nothing.

"We've got to go look," said the girl, tightly.

"But if they've just ditched in the muck," said Yellow Cap, "they'll radio for help, and everyone'll find us here. For nothing."

Tug flickered his ears about. He was hearing

another sound, faintly and not very distinctly. It began to seem like a human voice, with something not normal about it.

"Wait," the boy beside him hissed. "Tug's hearing something else. Listen."

"*Yes*," the girl said after a moment. "Oh, god, it's a cry for help. Come on, we've got to get there!"

"Hold it," Yellow Cap said sharply. "I'm no good on one leg. But I can ride this bike. I'll go call for help, 'cause maybe their radio's busted. You two go look what's needed now."

"Yes!" said the girl. "You won't have to say who you are or where you're calling from. It won't matter if they find *us*. We could be just out here on a lark. For Dad's sake, get out of here before they find you!"

Tug saw the girl swing away from the motorcycle. He heard Yellow Cap give another pained grunt as he slid awkwardly forward on the seat where she'd been. Then the motor's grumble stirred up, and the machine, with Yellow Cap, went bouncing steadily away.

Tug saw the girl come toward him. He watched with surprise as the boy boosted her up onto his back. Then Tug stood patiently as the boy pulled at his mane and clambered onto him again. When he felt a nudge, Tug started right toward the slough. The closer he got, the more distinctly he could hear that voice crying out so strangely. It kept his attention, and the howllike tone of it kept him alert, but that didn't stop him from pushing his old muscles into the heavy trot the boy urged. Because the closer he got, the richer the smell of that dampness. Tug trotted eagerly. He wanted to find a puddle to drink from.

19

The Desperate Connection

THIS TIME THEY WERE RIDing on Tug, not the motorcycle. This time she was behind him, clinging tightly to his waist. Staying on a trotting horse bareback was not easy, but Arley concentrated mostly on other emergencies. He wasn't anxious to see whatever he was going to see just ahead, or to endure what would occur, when more police came, as they would have to. Though probably not because that brother had called anyone. It seemed as likely that the guy would try to skip out of it completely.

Meanwhile, as Tug jogged them forward, the strained shouts for help became louder, and Arley thought to answer. "Coming!" he shouted.

"Here!" the panicked voice cried out, more strongly.

They came back along the shadowed trail to the slough, with the moonlit sky open above it. Under the sky-glow, the rough, weather-worn bridge timbers had a soft glow and looked like smooth iron, except now they were bent and sloped out of shape.

Arley reined Tug to a stop, and he and the girl each lifted a leg high and to the side and rapidly slid off together. As he ran down off the trail, Arley's stomach tightened, not knowing what horrible sight he was going to have to look at. He saw first that the girl had been right: the vehicle, in breaking down the old bridge, had not fallen straight through. It was tilted to one side, with the back end still hooked by one wheel to the bridge, and a front fender nosed down into the slough. Just back of that fender, he saw a nearly bald man on his knees scooping vigorously at the ground like a digging dog.

"Get a wedge!" the man gasped. "God, I thought it was made of steel. It'll kill him!"

But Arley figured he had to get closer to understand what was going on. By now the moon had risen high enough to be directly in the open sky above the slough, and it made the slough grasses brightly pale and the mud beneath them shadowy dark. In the shadow beneath the Bronco, Arley could make out the pale face and darker shoulder of another man, caught under the vehicle's front end.

The bald man, panting and wheezing, kept clawing up gobs of muck, and Arley realized that the Bronco's front end was steadily settling deeper into the soft bottom and would either crush or suffocate the trapped man beneath it. The digging man kept loosening just enough earth beneath his partner to give him breathing room, but the loosened earth was also letting that motor-heavy end of the Bronco sink faster.

"He tried to jump but fell beneath it. Get a wedge!" the digging man cried out.

"We'll need an axe," said the girl.

"In the vehicle!" the man grunted.

"I know," she answered. "I just looked, and if we open a door it might shake and drop completely off the bridge."

"Get a pole to brace it!" the man cried out, and he clawed again into the slough.

"That tongue—" Arley muttered, and quickly waded through the slough grasses to where they'd abandoned the sled. He grabbed the tongue and wrenched it this way and that, but couldn't get it loose from the sled. "We'd have to *chop* it free," he had to admit. And if, by moonlight, they could find in the woods any limbs or trunks that were big enough, and had fallen loose, they'd be probably too rotten.

"Hey, Gregg had an axe!" The girl had come behind him.

Together they jumped closer to the bolster beam that lay across the runners. Extra rope, intended to hold stolen packages to the bolster, was still tied there in coils—but no axe.

"Did he have it loose at the lake?" She tried to remember out loud. "Maybe you could ride—"

Arley was kicking at the grassy ground, seeing nothing and quickly giving up. It might not be at the lake. It could've fallen off anywhere. "C'mon," he said. "Let's use the whole sled as a brace. It seems solid."

But she held still and argued, "We can't. It's too bulky. It won't fit where it'll brace anything."

"What're you doing? Hurry up!" the bald man yelled as he struggled to keep digging beside the Bronco.

"We're hurrying!" she shouted to him.

But they weren't making a move.

"Axe-jack-saw-shovel—" With frustrated urgency Arley was snapping off the names of things they might use and couldn't name one they could get hold of.

"We need a crane. Go get a crane!" the digging man shouted. "There's got to be logging trucks around here." Logging trucks did have small loader cranes mounted on them. "Don't just stand there!"

"We're trying to think!" The girl answered him sharply with her own excitement. "There's no time to go—"

"Get those rope coils loose!" Arley commanded suddenly. "See if they'll reach to that edge of trees. Maybe there's a limb there. I'll get Tug." Then without waiting for any kind of answer he went plowing through the tall slough grass. His big horse was slowly wandering away, dragging the halter rope, plucking up bunches of grass, searching around for water deep enough to drink. Don't run from me now, Arley silently begged, and as usual Tug did not. He just stood and looked up with a thick moustache of grasses jiggling from his steadily grinding jaws.

"C'mon. You gotta help fast," Arley announced, while as smoothly as he could he took the halter rope, then headed back toward the vehicle as rapidly as he could, with Tug's big feet making squnching sounds right behind him and Tug's grassy breath close behind his head.

"A horse'll jerk it. Ride for a crane!" the bald man shouted at him. The man was fighting bare-handed for the friend's life right in front of him and knew it could soon be useless. His voice roared with frantic anger.

Arley could only repeat, "There's no time for a crane!" as he went tromping by.

"You can't just *pull* it, you gotta *lift it!* Or it'll fall on him!" the bald man yelled, and started to rise up for some furious purpose. Then he seemed to decide he didn't dare stop his scooping and went back down at it.

The girl had lined out the extra rope to the nearest edge of the slough and was leaping through mud coming back.

"It reaches the trees," she panted as she arrived. "You'd think there'd be limbs. But they're all too high or too thin."

"Aren't there any?" Arley snapped.

"I can see one. It's not the best."

"It'll *do*," Arley grunted.

He had the short ropes up in his hand, and she began helping him tie them back around Tug's neck. They'd been cut loose before and were now hardly long enough. Together they managed to knot them back together.

"You're going to run a rope from the Bronco over a limb," she said, understanding, "then down to Tug, so when he pulls he'll lift that front end up. But what if the rope binds over the limb too tightly to be pulled?"

"Then it'll wear through and break," Arley muttered.

"The rope'll stretch," she reminded him. "And that limb'll dip."

"And if we let it slack and jerk because of that the rope'll break!" Arley hissed. "But that Bronco's *sure* going to fall and kill him if we don't do something quick!"

"It's tipping more! We gotta lift it!" the bald man wailed.

"You're right," the girl breathed. "We'll *have* to try it."

"Lift it! Hurry!" the bald man yelled.

"We *will!*" the girl gave him an answer.

"Is he still *alive?*" Arley wanted to know.

"*Yes*. I see spit bubbling at his mouth!"

"Keep at it! We're hurrying!" Arley said, and went jumping across the mud as fast as he could, towing Tug behind him. At the edge of trees, he turned to ask the girl where the limb was, but she wasn't there. She hadn't followed him. He saw her already worming on her back by the Bronco, putting the other end of the long rope in under its low front end. If the rear wheels slipped off the bridge before she got the rope tied at the front and crawled away, her arms would be trapped underneath and she might be crushed too. Arley could not help her, or even take time to watch. He rushed his glance upward, searching for a limb, found there was only one that might work. He coiled the rope end, flung it up over the limb, caught the tip as it swung back down from the other side, and began tying it to

Tug's neck ropes. By then he could see the girl
standing up and looking as if she wanted to go help
the man digging, but not daring to get too close, not
knowing what his panic might make him do.

In fact the man abruptly got from both knees
up onto one knee and shifted awkwardly to one side.
"It's sinking lower!" he screamed. "I can't hardly
get my arms under. Get a crane and *lift* it! Don't
just gawk and let him die! You're killing him!"

There was no way to calm the man. No way to
do anything till they were ready to do it. Arley tried
to concentrate on what *he* knew had to be done.
"Hey, I need shirts for padding!" he realized, and
once more stripped off what was left of his own.
He was afraid that without some padding, the pain
of the cutting ropes would be so great Tug wouldn't
work smoothly.

The girl quickly tossed him hers. And from just
out of the bald man's reach she demanded he give
up his. She made just a quick step toward him, in-
sisting on getting his attention again. The bald man
hesitated. He seemed about to rise up, or yell again,
but had no spare breath for it. With a sudden gesture
of helpless rage he tore the buttons free and yanked
his arms out of his shirt, flung it aside and went back
to his desperate clawing at the mud.

No one said anything as Arley grabbed up the
shirt—it was some kind of thick uniform material—

and shoved all the cloth he now had under Tug's neck ropes.

Then he grabbed the halter rope. He wanted to talk to Tug, to explain that when he pulled, the weight wouldn't be right behind him, but would seem to be from a limb above, and that would be okay. But he *mustn't* jerk. Must set his feet so he didn't slip. Because if that Bronco was pulled off the bridge before their rope stretched tight, or if the rope snapped, there wouldn't be anything holding up the front end, and that man under there was done.

But Tug wouldn't understand talk; it might just distract him.

Arley realized his heart was pounding. He couldn't control it. But he had to control the rest of his muscles to make them move slowly, and evenly, or how would Tug understand to move so especially easy, too?

Gradually Arley reached one hand up the halter rope to take hold of the halter itself. He'd have to have a close hold, so he'd have a chance to control Tug, no matter what the mud underfoot, or that rope or limb, or that Bronco started to do. Suppose Tug just couldn't hold enough of the Bronco's weight?

"*Slowly—*" Arley began talking to Tug in spite of himself.

With one hand clenching the halter, Arley

eased a foot forward. Tug began to step, too. The narrow gray reflection of the moonlight on the rope began to grow brighter as the coarse strands slowly began to stretch and became more rigid. . . .

20

Tug's Excavation

TUG STARTED SLOWLY TO move forward, for that was how the boy directed him to move. Right away Tug felt that there was nothing behind him, that the load seemed to be above him. That must be wrong so he stopped. The boy urged him slowly on, so he started again.

As the tow rope began to grow taut upward, Tug realized that whatever load he was tied to was much heavier than the sled he'd been pulling, even with a man on it. The coarse ropes around his neck, with the bumps from the extra knots, started to cut through the weak padding of the shirt cloth. They began to be like slowly rubbing saw blades where his skin was already raw from dragging the sled.

Because of the pain, Tug didn't want to pull any more. He tried to stop, but right away the boy urged him slowly on. The boy was steadier and much more familiar to him than Yellow Cap had been, and the clear pain didn't frighten Tug the way the dark threat of having to jump off the truck had. Tug was much too used to hauling and obeying to stop just because of the pain. He began to pull harder, to start taking a step forward, despite the ropes tearing into him. It was a short step, for though the boy kept urging him to move, the boy's hands kept a tight grip on the halter.

"*The rope's stretching,*" the boy whispered. "*So you can't stop—'cause that'll jerk—*"

The squeeze of the neck ropes kept getting tighter. Because the towline went up over the limb the pressure didn't go against Tug's shoulders; it got worse and worse around his neck. He found it hard to breathe, and that was frightening; he tried to stop, but the familiar boy's steady voice and hands quickly urged him to go on.

So Tug gradually kept pulling harder, despite having to cough for breath, despite the smell of his own blood as it began to squeeze out around the neck ropes and streak down his hair.

Suddenly, behind him, a swift scraping screech began, and before it finished, the rope yanked heavily backward. To ease the jolt against his neck, Tug instantly raised his head high, lifting the boy, who still clung to his halter, right off the ground. But Tug's big hooves dug in and gave not an inch. In that combination of yielding a little but mostly staying put, he kept the rope from snapping and didn't let it go limp.

"What's *happened?*" the boy shouted as he hung below Tug's ears.

"The back end came down off the bridge!" The girl's voice rang out behind him.

"It sank on him!" the bald man cried out, from flat in the mud. "No. No!" the tone of his voice changed. "It didn't. I can see he's all right. The rope's still holding. The front end's not on the ground."

Arley now had one hand on the halter, and one on Tug's mane, as Tug slowly forced his head down, though that pulled the new grips of the ropes even tighter.

"*Easy—hold it—don't let it go slack!*" the boy whispered as his feet touched earth. Then away from Tug he shouted, "Can you get him out?"

"We're going to dig!" the girl called back.

"Don't let loose of that rope!" the bald man exclaimed.

So Tug didn't have to try again to move the strange load. But the boy kept him pulling against the biting and choking neck ropes, so the towline would stay taut and hold the front end of the Bronco from weighing down on the man underneath it. In order to do that, while staying in one place, Tug had to constantly pull his sinking feet out of the ooze. He had to keep wading, though going nowhere, while the ropes burned harshly and squeezed his breath, while ever more mosquitoes discovered his flowing blood and the boy's bare back and gathered around them both.

"Don't let loose of that rope!" The bald man's voice sounded blunt and hollow, for only his legs could be seen, and the girl's beside his, squirming on the ground in the moonlight. Both of them were half under the Bronco, clawing and gouging with their hands, trying to dig a trough by which to gently pull the trapped man out.

"*They're all under there now,*" the boy whispered to Tug. "*We've got to keep it tight—or we'll kill them all.*"

Tug's ears flickered toward the whispers. His body heaved as he pumped hard for air. He was hurting, but sensed nothing for him to be alarmed about. Calmly he let each foot sink into the mud, then exerted himself to pull it out, and set it down again in the same place, steadily leaning against the ropes, working his way still toward more food, and *water.*

The airplane went by, low overhead, a quick,

dark shape droning fiercely, without even a tiny blinking light. Tug ignored it. The sound quickly faded into the treetop noises of the breeze.

Meanwhile the bald man's voice began to change again. *"Easy,"* he muttered, with a softer but still hollow sound. *"Easy*—steady—*straight*—easy—*steady*—" he kept speaking, breathless himself, but clearer and clearer. Then the plane went darkly over a second time, blacked-out as a caution against being shot at by dangerous hidden smugglers. "—straight—*easy*—steady—steady . . . Okay!" the bald man exclaimed. "He's out. He's out! We've got him! Don't move him any more!"

"He's so *pale*," the girl's voice was worried.

"He's *alive*," the bald man said. "He's in shock. Get him warm. We need an ambulance. The radio!—"

At the same time the front end of the Bronco settled down into the slough, because Tug had been allowed to step back and relax.

"Good job! Good job!" Tug heard the boy's steady voice still whispering; a knife flickered again in the moonlight, and again the biting neck ropes let loose and fell away. Behind them there was a metallic creaking from one of the Bronco's doors. The boy ignored that and tried to peer closer at Tug's galled neck.

Then the bald man shouted: "The radio's dead. Get that horse and go for help!"

Tug didn't understand any of the words, or why there was still more excitement. But as the boy grabbed his mane and began clambering onto his back again, Tug held still, and then obeyed and turned about as the boy's pull on the halter rope ordered. The bald man, dripping mud, was yanking a blanket and first aid kit from the Bronco as Tug waded near him. The girl was kneeling over the wounded man they'd pulled free. She stood up, looking like a living statue made of mud, and Tug was stopped beside her.

"When you get to the road, turn left a half mile. There's a house. The name's Bradley Phillips, they have a phone. And you two were great," she said. "*Great.*"

"You had guts to go under there," the boy said. "I still wouldn't want to follow you everywhere."

"Go get help!" the bald man yelled at close range, and right away Tug was ordered forward again, out of the slough and up onto the trail—there he raised his head and flickered his ears, and with his breath no longer squeezed, he sniffed deeply at the air, for something else was approaching.

The boy noticed his signals and let him pause. Another glow began to appear down the long opening of the old road. "Someone's coming!" the boy reported, before the bald man could yell again to get going. The light grew jerkily brighter and closer. A rattling of metal and the bumping of wheels became more distinct.

Soon a large farm tractor arrived, with large hydraulic tines, used for loading hay, protruding out in front, and chains wrapped loosely around those tines.

"Where did *you* come from?" The bald man spoke out in astonishment.

"Heard there was a wreck. Maybe someone hurt," said the man on the tractor.

"We need a doctor and ambulance," the bald man said.

"They're on their way," the tractor man replied.

"Brad, who got you?" the girl called out.

"Why—it is you, Phyllis. It was your brother. He came gunning that motorcycle into our yard instead of waking your dad, and—"

"Where is Gregg now?"

"Out by the tracks to wave down any train and guide in the medics. There's some cops coming too. Supposed to have a plane up there looking for my lights, to radio directions. Seems like there's more going on out here than at the fair. Who's hurt?"

"We're Border Patrol," said the bald man.

"How can I help?" asked the tractor man.

"See if you can pull our rig out," said the bald man. "If it'll run again, we may have to use it as an ambulance as far as the road. C'mon!"

Tug felt the boy slide off and watched him go with the others, all of them grouping around the two machines. Tug was alone. At first he began shaking his head, stomping his feet, vibrating all the muscles just below his skin, trying to shake loose the burning ache that the ropes had left. And he tried to rub the ache off against the brush. But he could not escape it. So he did the next best thing: he took in a mouthful of leaves and began to munch them, waiting for the pains to go away.

As he reached for another mouthful, he realized he wasn't tied. So he began to move, dragging the halter rope back toward the tantalizing smell of moisture in the slough. The smell was stronger now. It led him right back to where he'd stood leaning against the sharp ropes and treading his feet to keep from sinking in too deeply. He'd churned up a big wide hole there, and it was filling with water. It was dark water, but clean water, water that had been flowing beneath the surface. It tasted a little like the bark of old trees, but it was cool and very smooth and wet. Tug stood, with his big feet spread wide and his head down, calmly sipping it as it came.

FIVE

Doing Different Things Differently

21

Not All News
Is in the Papers

THE SEVENTH DAY OF AU-
gust was the next publication day of the Feast Lake
weekly newspaper; and one of the tallest, oldest
horses in the country had his picture in it, on the
front page, right amid a parade of other pictures
showing different winners of prizes at the Timber
County Fair. But the story about Tug talked of
other things.

"Look what's written here—" Arley's mom said.
She was coming in with the mail as Arley and his
dad were starting out after lunch. "It says that
'Smugglers stole a top pulling horse from the County

Fair to help haul their goods in from a plane on a local lake. But Phyllis and Gregg Bettmann, of Rune, saw them steal it and got its owner, fourteen-year-old Arley Rawlinson of Feast Lake, and they chased after the thieves on a motorcycle. They not only got the horse back, but used the horse to save the life of a border patrolman who was injured while rounding up the gang.' That's not exactly what happened. Is it?"

"No. Not exactly," said Arley. "But it keeps her brother's name out of trouble."

"They had to write something about it," said his dad. "And you know they couldn't call Gregg Bettmann a crook. Besides maybe giving his father another stroke, they might've got sued for libel, since no one's going to prosecute him."

"I still don't know how you talked that county attorney out of it," said Mom. When Arley had called them at dawn last Saturday, saying he'd had a wild night and asking them to come almost to Rune to pick him and Tug up, she, of course, had gone with her husband. But because of farm chores needing to be done every day, she hadn't been at every meeting that had been held since then.

"Not just the *county* people," said Dad. "Smuggling's a *federal* crime."

"Either way," said Mom. "I never thought *I'd*

be agreeing to let a person go who steals a horse and deliberately plans to kill it."

"Well, like we told them," said Arley, "he didn't really go through with anything but the stealing. And he didn't duck out from calling for the medics, even when he was plenty scared of getting caught."

"He just didn't ever seem mean underneath," said Dad. "Just young and excitable and got off on the wrong foot. And we're not exactly letting him go. This deal we've made won't hurt us, and maybe it'll straighten him out."

"I keep hoping so," said Mom. "But it'll bear watching."

Dad nodded. "I know. But at least now we'll have an idea of *who* to watch. Does it also say anything about this Saturday coming?"

"Well, wait—there's so many pictures, most of the stories are on the inside pages." Mom had the rest of the mail clamped between an elbow and her body and it was starting to slip out as she tried to open the paper. Dad reached and took the mail and set it on the table among the empty plates.

"This is all prize lists," Mom murmured. "Let's see . . . Here they tell about that airplane: 'Four people were arrested loading it in Canada earlier that afternoon.'"

"We heard there were three," said Arley.

"It says four now."

"The newspaper probably asked more people than we did," said Dad. "So they probably got a different set of facts."

"It says one of the men is from Feast Lake," Mom added.

"That's that pilot friend of Gregg's," said Arley.

"Then they explain how the Border Patrol flew the plane down here, hoping to catch the rest of the gang when they met it, but ended up using it to guide the ambulance to that logging trail."

"But what about this *coming* Saturday?" Arley wanted to know.

"Here it is! I thought it was an ad, they put such a thick black line around it. It says, 'Tug, the big timber horse who was the central figure in last weekend's smuggling attempt, had earlier put on a special demonstration of skilled log-snaking at the fairgrounds. It's reported it was this skill that convinced the smugglers they should steal him for their use. On Saturday, August ninth, he'll be displaying his skills again, legally, in two special benefit performances at the Birch County Fair in Mendavia. Proceeds will help provide rehabilitation treatment for George Bettmann, of Rune, a recent stroke victim.' "

"What about the state fair and that Wild Rice Festival at Corley?" Arley asked.

Mom, holding the paper up like a sail in a breeze, turned it to another two pages, and after scanning those, folded it over to the back page, which was all an ad of thank-yous for help different people and companies did at the Feast Lake fair. "No," she reported. "Nothing. But those calls only came yesterday, and the state fair's not a sure thing yet."

"Good," said Arley. "The more separate stories we get, the more people'll know about it and come to watch. I hope we can draw enough money."

"You ought to get five hundred people willing to pay a dollar to watch at Mendavia. Maybe even twice that," said Dad. "Gene Carr can sure arrange these things. He's got all the 4-H clubs in the council making advertising posters for Mendavia and Corley both. And there'll be more people at Corley. You said he's also been phoning other county agents asking about other shows you could go to. Once you get started, I bet he finds more places that are interested. Even if you don't make it to state, I bet you draw in several thousand dollars before you quit being festival stars."

"You're sure those rope burns on Tug'll be healed enough for him to work on Saturday?" Mom asked. Ever since they'd had their herd take disastrously sick on the plains, she'd been keeping double and triple tabs on any animal injured or ill.

"We've got good harness here," Dad reminded her. "We can pad it good enough for him to pull just a show log."

"And I bet Tug's going to enjoy having new things to do," said Arley.

Mom folded the paper up smaller and put it out of her way, saying as she did, "Meanwhile I guess we ought to enjoy the fact that Arley and Tug got home safe, and that we're all healthy enough to do things."

"*Meanwhile* . . ." said Dad, "we'd better be out and doing them. We've got to be ready to go when they get here. So Arley'll have time to visit with his girl friend."

"She's not my girl friend, so lay off," said Arley. "She's two years older, remember."

"Well, when you're ten years older, that won't make a bit of difference," Dad kept teasing.

"Talk to me about it then," said Arley.

"Okay, if you remind me." Dad laughed. "But right now we have some fence posts to get cut."

"*That's* what I got up from the table for." Arley grinned.

22

Help Arrives

THIS TIME THE TRUCK crossed the gray cement bridge first—over the creek where the cranberries grew so well—and then without stopping went slowly past the woods in which they'd roused the bear on their spying expedition in mid-July.

This time Phyllis was driving and Gregg sat on the right side, with his yellow cap pulled down squarely, and one pants leg split open to fit around the white plaster cast that encased his hurt knee.

This time the truck bed, though practically empty, smelled of trampled straw and cow manure, for they had spent most of yesterday hauling their dairy cattle to the sale barn at Feast Lake. With the money from selling their cattle, added to what the benefit log-pulls would bring, they were hoping the costs of their father's treatments, which were now scheduled to begin on Monday, could be met without selling their farm. As soon as his cast was off, Gregg would look for winter's work with a logging outfit. Their pastures, which had good fencing already in place, they would rent to the Rawlinsons, and in the meantime they would donate their labor to cutting and setting fence posts around the Rawlinsons' land.

The deal had already been worked out with the Rawlinsons, and the different government attorneys and police were acting as if they'd go along with it. But still Gregg sat stiffly, staring ahead, his jaw clamped tensely.

"Relax," Phyllis murmured to him. "Everything's arranged, and I haven't run this off the road yet."

"I wouldn't care if you did," he murmured. "I could fix the truck."

"Well, we're going to fix everything else." She tried to cheer him. "Dad's stroke, and what you did by stealing their horse."

"*We*'re going to fix it," Gregg grumbled. "You mean you and your boyfriend."

"He's not my boyfriend."

"You talk about him enough."

"We did some things that night worth talking about. We started out as clawing strangers and ended up as tough-working partners. It can happen again. With you."

Then they were past the woods. The Rawlinsons' stumpy clearing opened out to one side.

Gregg turned to his sister. "Look," he said uncomfortably. "I still don't know how I'm just going to get out and say, 'Hi,' to people I've tried to rob. And I don't like taking charity."

"It's something besides charity," she insisted. "Arley's going to have a lot of fun putting on those shows. And with our pastures to use, they can spend the money they've saved to buy their new beef cows. They won't have to spend it all just on a lot of fencing that won't produce any calves they can sell. When Dad's treatments are done, we'll have their ground fenced. Then we can start saving to buy new cows to put back on our pastures, and we'll all be doing what we want."

By then she was driving even slower and turning into the Rawlinsons' driveway. "What I wish," she added, "is that we'd figured out something like this to start with. Look—they're ready and waiting . . . Hello! Here we are. Ready to start." She spoke out the window as she eased the truck to a stop.

Arley's dad came over to her window. "Right on time," he said. "And glad to see you. It's going to be a pleasant change for us to have some extra hands working."

"We plan to help it go easier," Phyllis said.

"Oh, I don't doubt you can," said Arley's dad. "And more fun too. The only question is how well can Gregg move that leg around today?"

Gregg was hearing enough relaxed enthusiasm in their talk that he took the chance and joined in. With a sudden burst of spirit, he spoke up for himself: "I bet I can prop myself and trim limbs off all the posts you guys cut."

"Good enough," Arley's dad answered. "We'll feed 'em to you."

23

Tug Keeps at It

Tug's neck and shoulders were all splotchy blue from the medicine that had been put on to keep flies off his cuts so they could heal. But Tug wasn't giving any attention to how he looked. He was standing in his neatly cleaned shed only because there were fewer midday flies in the shade than out in the paddock. He heard a vehicle arriving, and there was something vaguely familiar to its rumble, yet he paid it little attention either, till he heard Yellow Cap's voice come strongly through the air.

Then Tug stirred about a little uneasily and looked out alertly. He didn't want to meet with Yellow Cap again, but could think of nothing to do but keep watching with interest. He saw the people get into both of the trucks that were now in the yard and go off on an old narrow, bumpy single-lane that led through the stumps toward an edge of the woods that was thick with slender cedar trees. Soon from that direction Tug heard the sounds of a chain saw and chopping axes.

He didn't realize it was merely fence posts being cut. He began plodding about, restlessly. It didn't matter to him that he was healing. Without anything pressing against them, his shoulders felt all well. And idleness with the sounds of work around him made him uneasy. He wanted to begin pulling, because when he did that and it was over, there was always new feed and water and rest. He'd been resting steadily for five days in a row; and without work in between, the rest didn't feel nearly as good. It was unusual. There were no beginnings and endings, and he wasn't yet used to that.

In the distance the sawing and chopping continued. Tug now moved steadily about his paddock, shaking off flies, not getting any hauling done, but at leasting working up a good fresh strong appetite.